Dirty X-mas Boo

A Fake Dating Holiday Romantic
Mystery

Missy Terrell

PEARLFECTIONIST(A)

The number 4 is a Hallmark of good things...love my ivies.

Contents

Prologue

THE BOY COULD BE heard wailing for miles. People walking by took a look at the child and the tears that drenched his face and shook their heads as they walked on. There was nothing to be done for him. Rather there was nothing to be done for the puppy in his arms that was clearly fighting for its last breath.

The boy was about five, no more than six. The puppy was just that, all big feet and ears, the awkward stage where some of the animal grew and waited for the rest of the body to catch up.

A few of the people had seen the dog be struck by a car, but the car had long since left. The driver didn't speed off, only trundling along without pausing. Uncaring. In fact, it appeared as though the driver was blissfully unaware of having hit the small puppy. It was just another animal after all.

To the boy, it was his world, his love laid out in blood and torn fur. The dog was in agony, that was plain to see, but the poor thing was too weak and too hurt to protest the frantic groping of his boy, the tears shed from the child fell and mixed in with blood-stained fur.

"Where is his mother?"

"Poor thing."

Sympathetic murmurs from the few pedestrians fell on the child like judgements and the puppy tried to raise its head for a final kiss to his companion.

"Mon chien! S'il vous plait!" He could barely get the words out through the sobbing. His nose and cheeks became pink from his distress. His companion was about to die in his arms.

A pair of shoes, brightly shined, black leather stopped in front of him. A woman's pair of shoes, a swirling skirt at his eye level. The woman took one knee in front of him and lay a hand on the puppy's head. She was beautiful and moved with a cat like grace. Her face was kind, her breath was soothing, but her eyes held secrets, mysteries that the boy could not understand. He would have been frightened of her, might have run from that gaze, but he would not leave his friend. Whatever fate the puppy was to have would be shared. That much he could give the dog, if nothing else.

"He's dying." She repeated the words in French when the English seemed to make no impact. She might have been commenting on the weather. Hearing it put so baldly, so dispassionately made it real somehow and the boy forgot how to breathe.

"Madame?" He didn't know what he was begging for, there was nothing to be done, even at his tender age, he knew it was over for the dog. He screwed up his face and begged her in her own language. "*Please.*"

"What's your name boy? *Comment t'appelle*?" She whispered the question, cupping his face between her hands to gain his full attention.

Seeing that there was now an adult who was taking the matter into her own hands, the rest of the crowd ignored them and continued in their journeys, content that it was someone else's problem.

"François." The boy swallowed hard. "François."

"I am Madame Isabelle." The lady raised an eyebrow as though she expected him to know that name. When he seemed bewildered, she reached out to caress his head and then touched the muzzle of the gasping dog.

"You love this little one, yes?"

The boy François nodded, his fingers clutching the rough fur of the puppy.

She took a breath and glanced around her. Contented that they were no longer the center of attention, she continued. "What will you give me?"

François didn't understand and his expression must have shown that. She tried again. "You need to pay for things, boy. What do you have for me?"

He would have said anything. Everything. He would have gladly put himself in thrall to save the puppy. He dug into his pockets and pulled out everything he had. Bottle caps and rocks and shining coins and feathers and what might have been a genuine arrowhead. This was the summation of a summer's worth of exploration and mischief. It was everything he could count as his and his alone.

She looked over the collection with a skeptical eye. Long, tapered fingers with bright red nail polish that looked remarkably like the blood on the matted fur hovered over his collection and gingerly picked a shining agate and a crow's feather. She hesitated over the rest, finally choosing one of his quarters, leaving the other two behind.

Her fee vanished into a purse and her hands began moving again, this time, over the whimpering puppy.

From the corner of his eye, he watched the magic unfold. White threads that were both there and not there at the same time. It was a ghostly phantom, a trick of the light that gathered in her fingers and moved to her commands, obeying her gestures as she traced the injured puppy.

The trails wrapped around the dog and settled into the broken body. The dog sighed, it was a sound of relief, of contentment and the dog's body twitched.

She gathered more of the ghostly thread and wove it into the dog. Bone snapped and reformed in his grip and the boy gawked at the transformation. The puppy opened its eyes and blinked, no longer in distress. It licked its lips and the woman lay her hand flat over the dog, pressing the threads into the fur. The bald patches, the torn skin, the evidence of the car all seemed to wash away under her gestures and the puppy began to wag its tail.

She sat back and braced her fingers on the sidewalk. She seemed older, or perhaps...hollowed. The thread had clearly demanded something from her to do her bidding and she was silent for a long moment. She opened her eyes again and smiled. This time, the smile reached her eyes.

The puppy wriggled under his grasp and broke free of the boy's hands. It barked once and set its paws on the boy's shoulders, licking away the trail of tears on the dusty face.

François hugged the little dog fiercely and buried his face in the rough fur around the puppy's neck. He wept again, tears of relief, of joy. The dog squirmed and sensing his boy's distress wriggled into him to soothe his upset, his tongue everywhere at once.

"*Merci...*" Francios began, but the lady was gone. She had vanished as she had arrived, seeming to melt away into nothing at all. He searched behind him, down the street and into the nearby stores, but she was nowhere to be found.

He gathered the remaining possessions from the sidewalk and shoved them back into his pockets. The puppy was jumping at his feet and ready to resume their adventures. This time, François double checked the leash and wrapped it around one pudgy fist. He wasn't going to let go again. Never.

He wiped his face on his sleeve, taking off the tears and dog slobber and swallowed hard. Even at his age, he knew that what just happened wasn't possible. This Madame Isabelle had done something no one should have been able to do. She had gifted him a miracle.

And shown him something new.

He sat down again on the curb, the puppy sitting attentively at his side.

She had called the threads.

François concentrated and moved his hands the way she had. To his delight a small thread of white followed his gestures. Something stung inside as he pulled it, tugging at a place he could not put a name to. It was not painful, but it took something from him.

You need to pay for things.

Yes. That made sense.

He decided the puppy was worth paying for and tied one end of the thread to the dog's collar and then brought the other end to his wrist and gently wrapped it around. The thread was cold and brought a chill to his wrist, but it didn't hurt too much.

The puppy concentrated on his boy. François felt as though they understood each other in a way they hadn't experienced before. The thread joined them.

He walked the dog home in silence. He spent the time thinking about the day. When he got to the abandoned factory where he lived with the others, he took off the physical leash, but the puppy never left his side. Not until he reached out to untie the thread and the dog happily bolted across the building, chasing rats and barking shrilly at the other children who drew back, as if sensing something about the dog was different now.

Changed.

François flicked his fingers and the thread floated away, back to wherever it came.

It barely even stung anymore.

Chapter 1

Francois

F RANCOIS WAS CERTAIN HE was going to hell. Celebrating Christmas by getting a gift from a voodoo shop had to be some sort of Catholic sin. Maybe one not officially recognized by the church, but one all the same.

Still, what do you buy for a young couple that has everything including supernatural problems? Voodoo dolls? The trinkets that they had on display was the sort of thing some older person from the Midwest would buy and show off to her bridge club as a memento to the "dark underside" of New Orleans. Not that it was even close to the real thing. Since that old movie came out about the backpackers searching for a witch, it seemed anyone could take a few twigs and scrap of cloth and call it an evil voodoo doll.

Honestly, the store was mostly tourist nonsense, but where else could one find the sort of thing that just said 'Merry Christmas' in a voodoo kind of way? He picked up a crystal ball and tried to imagine the look on their faces when they unwrapped that. He decided he didn't much like the thought and set it back carefully. The thing was heavy enough to so some serious damage. He gazed into it in case there was a message the ball wanted to tell him, but all he saw was a fish-eye view of the store. Until something changed in the reflection and he stood quickly to see for himself just what...or who...was moving around behind him.

A most beautiful woman was shopping with one eyebrow raised in what he could only describe as a mixture of confusion and amusement. She took an interest in something and gingerly picked it up to get a closer look.

"Snakeskin." Francois said, trying to help. She made a face and dropped it back on the counter. "Not to worry," he assured her with a smile, "no snakes were harmed. It simply no longer wanted it."

She smiled back at him. "When it comes to snakes, my stance on not harming animals is somewhat...relaxed."

"*Mon dieu.* I have to agree. There is something about snakes that makes my skin crawl." He gingerly poked at the dropped skin. "Almost as much as this fellow's. *no?*"

She paused a moment. He'd seen that look before. She was trying to fix the accent. "Creole." He took her hand and lifted it, bending over her fingers dramatically. He brought the hand to his face, but did not kiss it, keeping eye contact the entire time.

"*Je suis* Francois." He let the hand fall and took a half step backward. "I see I am not the only one wishing someone a Merry Christmas in this..." he waved at the store, his usual silver tongue at a loss for a good description, "...place."

She laughed then. "No, no you're not, though I think you may have an advantage over me. I didn't even know what it was I was holding until you pointed it out."

He pulled a handkerchief from a pocket and offered it to her. "If you wish, *mademoiselle,* I would be honored to be of some small service in this regard."

She blushed then but refused his offer. "No, I'm recovered enough, I think, but thank you."

He set the kerchief back in his pocket and bowed slightly. "As for advantage, I have to disagree. I have no idea what sort of gift I want to get here. In fact, I would say I was at a disadvantage. I have disclosed my name, but you've not told me yours. This puts me at a distinct disadvantage and is quite sad as well."

She gave him a look that said she was on to his attempt to pick her up, but she wasn't offended by it. She looked him over and pursed her lips in thought. "Désirée."

"Charming Désirée." Her voice was light and silky to his ears. He muttered to himself but loud enough that she might hear him, "Desired, I agree." Then, he moved just close enough to the edge of her personal space narrowly avoiding invading it. The creamy chocolate of her cheeks deepened as she blushed again. "May I ask what you had in mind for a gift? This place caters to tourists, but if you look hard enough, there are some gems hidden under the trinkets made in China."

"I really don't know. I have a friend who is deeply interested in all this," She waved at the varied collection.

"As do I, though I confess, I was raised around it, so I do have a slight advantage. Does your friend do card readings?" He nodded toward a few decks beside them.

Désirée was unclear about what her 'friend' was actually interested in, but it soon came out after several careful questions that this friend did not hold a casual interest in the odd souvenir, but was engaged in a serious immersion into the occult. They spent a pleasurable hour discussing items before finding a blank journal with the words "MY SPELL BOOK" printed upon the cover as a joke gift and silver candle set for the real thing. She also eventually chose an antique wall clock, though why such a thing was in a voodoo shop, neither of them was able to determine.

Unfortunately his own shopping would have to wait for another day. He no longer had the proper concentration to sort the matter out, and honestly, he was more interested in spending time with the lovely Désirée.

Except now that the shopping was done it was time to leave.

Or at least time to leave the store.

Not that he didn't try to linger for as long as he could. They had examined the merchandise twice, mostly as an excuse to be together and prolong the experience as much as they could. "At least let me buy the clock, a present for you to remember this night by," Francois said, his fingers trailing along her arm, leaving a line of goosebumps.

"How is it a gift from me if you are the one doing the buying?" she asked laughing.

"Fair enough. But perhaps another memento perhaps?"

But Désirée flatly refused even the smallest item from the store. "Trust me, I highly doubt it's possible to forget a man such as you."

As far as flirtations went, it was quite satisfying. And about to be rudely interrupted as they were being watched.

The elderly woman wandering through the store looked hauntingly familiar to Francois, but she only smiled in that way older people do when they see fresh love. She seemed kind enough. She wore a small feather in her hair that was decidedly old, it was most likely a remembrance piece from someone or something important to her.

Harmless, he told himself, though she gave him an uneasy feeling whenever she ventured close. This more than anything let him know it was past time to leave.

"Shall we continue this elsewhere?" he asked, guiding her to the register where she made her purchases with Francois leaning against the counter, alert to every customer. He would not relax until they were outside.

Francois and Désirée continued together to the door. He topped her on the sidewalk, lingering though the night air was chill. "To be very honest, I do not wish this time to end."

"I agree." Her eyes were dark with unspoken promises. "You've made this fun."

Mon dieu but she was beautiful.

"This policy you have on harming of animals, does it extend to a perfect steak, rare with succulent mushrooms and a port sauce that will make your tongue dissolve?"

She bit her lip as she considered the question. "Sounds wonderful, to be honest."

"Fine then." Francois fairly glowed. "*Bonne Nourriture*at 7 tomorrow night. I will be the handsome man in the corner looking for a beautiful woman."

"*Bonne...*"

"*Bonne Nourriture*. It is in the French Quarter."

"Seven." Désirée smiled and ducked her head almost coyly. Francois thought it was a most fetching habit of hers. He again took her hand, and this time, he kissed the back of it as he had wanted to do before.

"*Au revoir.*"

"*Au revoir, Francois.*"

Never was it so difficult to turn and walk away from a woman. The very air itself seemed full of promise, a silent song of promise that this was someone he should pay very close attention to. All the same, he turned and walked away, only because he could find no other excuse to linger. His car was in the opposite direction of where he was walking but it would look the fool to turn around now. He strolled down the block a bit, giving her enough time to gather herself and go before he trudged back to his car.

Sometimes, playing it cool involved taking some extra steps.

Not everyone understood that.

Chapter 2

Désirée

Lydia Rothschild would be the making or the breaking of her.

Désirée hadn't expected to be headed to Baton Rouge earlier than Thursday. Instead, here she was on the road a full two days earlier than expected. Normally, she would never have agreed to a client rearranging her schedule in such a high-handed manner. Lydia though...was special.

"No, she thinks she's special and we all kowtow to her, which only reinforces the *strong* opinion she holds of herself."

"Des, she can't be as bad as all that." Kendis' voice on the speaker phone came out a little tinny, and hard to hear. Reception on this stretch of highway wasn't proving good. One more annoyance to add to the day.

"Honey, you're my best friend, meaning I don't usually call you on it when you're off base. But right now, you're so far off I'm going to have to correct you. In love of course, because of the aforementioned friendship. She is precisely as bad as all that. Don't you ever think otherwise."

Kendis laughed, a good sound to hear since her friend hadn't been doing much laughing lately. "Are you warning me?"

Des checked her mirror before moving into the other lane to pass a slow-moving car. "I most assuredly am. When that man of yours wins his election, that woman will cross his path, and you need to be ready for her."

"Duly noted. Now tell me about this thing you're planning for her. I know it's some big gala affair, but you never gave me any of the details. It all came up very fast."

"Apparently, she only does things fast, which is why I'm going up early. She wants me to add a few extra events to lead up to the ball itself. A luncheon. Some kind of mixer. 12 Days of Christmas for the guests, her assistant said. I expect she'll have details for me when I arrive." She hit the turn signal and moved back into her lane just in time. An oncoming car went by horn blaring. She made a face at it in the mirror. She'd had plenty of room.

"Des, tell me you're not driving the way you usually do..."

"I only know one way to drive," she informed Kendis tartly, as if she hadn't just taken the exit perhaps a bit faster than necessary. Of course, if she'd seen the sign sooner, she might have been able to get over faster.

At least she would be there soon. She'd been seeing signs for the resort for the last few miles. "I'd better go, I think I see the place. You sent that message I asked you to? The note was dropped off at the restaurant to cancel my date?"

"It's the first time I've ever seen you fail to get a man's number. He must have been something."

Des thought about the handsome stranger she'd seen in the voodoo shop yesterday. He was a man who clearly knew his way around the best things French. His presence was jovial but while she couldn't put her gel manicure on it, there was more to him. "*Something* doesn't begin to cover it. Gotta go. We'll talk later."

With that Des disconnected just as the car rolled under the portico at the entrance to the restored plantation house which had the reputation as one of the most exclusive hotels in Baton Rouge. A valet sprang seemingly out of nowhere to take her car.

Well. This might be more interesting than she originally had thought.

***

Des liked nice things. For years she'd made a practice of making sure she had the right clothes, the right shoes, was ready with the right impression. Her mother had taught her that first impressions were everything.

This place…was giving her all the wrong impressions from the moment she stepped through the door.

A rack of brochures advertising 'ghost tours' and something called a 'midnight haunted adventure' was the first thing she saw when she came in. A book about the plantation and hotel's history held the subtitle of "Most haunted location in Louisiana" which certainly didn't bode well for her stay.

Not that Des necessarily believed in ghosts, still she was raised to respect the possibility. This was all just a little more occult than she'd planned on for a holiday extravaganza. Now she was wondering if she needed to rethink her theme over to something a little less 'Christmas Dreams Come True' and a little more 'Christmas Carol' – the version with the creepiest ghosts which gave her nightmares as a child. She shivered spontaneously.

Perhaps she would have been a little more reassured had there not been a distinct feeling of not being alone in her room. Between the bathroom door closing when she was not anywhere near it and the way her room key kept leaping off the dresser, the place seemed a little too restless for her tastes.

She stood a long moment in the middle of her room, hands fisted on her hips as around her items spun, clattered and moved on their own volition. "I did not sign up for this."

Well, she had. Kind of. Only she didn't have time for this. Not when it was time to meet her employer and the manager of the property.

Mr. Martin Quinn was waiting for her at the bottom of the stairs. "How are you finding your room?" he asked by way of greeting. "Everything quiet?"

She stared at him a long moment. Mr. Quinn was the affable type, all smiles, well-practiced in the art of pleasing guests. He was also a little too curious, as though her being in that particular room was a test of sorts.

"All's about as I expected," she replied. "Where might I find Mrs. Rothschild? I expect she'll want to be part of the tour."

"She will join us in the dining room after I have shown you around."

Des nodded though inwardly it annoyed her that she was being put off. The reason for the tour though became more apparent once Mr. Quinn had shown her around a bit. "It's a bit of a winding house. There were several additions built on over the years, and as you see, the design of the hotel makes it somewhat difficult to get around sometimes From the outside you can see the difference in the roofing but navigating the inside...can be more or less challenging. For example, as you can see this dining room can be closed off with those doors there to create a smaller, more intimate dining space, but it makes it difficult to access the other half of the dining room. You'd have to go out and around through there." He pointed toward a door which turned out to lead to a back hallway. "At one point, it was used by the servants, and, truly, even today, usually only the staff will use them to get around. Thankfully the rooms don't get shut off like this often, but it can be cumbersome. Especially if you're trying to set up different events at one time. Likewise, the ballroom can be similarly divided using the long accordion doors between."

She stared at him. "Just how many events can you run here at one time then?"

"As many as we need."

The rest of the tour passed by in a blur. She was shown the kitchens only briefly, a door which led to the basement, and a different door which took one to the sub-basement, which was different from the basement. One of them was where the fuse boxes and the routers were set up. The other was where you'd find the laundry and clean linens. She had no idea which was which. The fact she was shown both was not exactly encouraging.

"It's an old building," Mr. Quinn said when she asked. "Things sometimes don't function the way they're supposed to. At such times you might be called upon to step in simply because you are the nearest one to effecting a solution."

"Peachy."

Outside she got an even briefer tour of the garden, saw a line of bungalows which families could rent out, and, even more interesting, the caretaker's cabin.

Mr. Quinn paused when he saw her interest. "That particular building is original to the plantation, older than the house itself which burned in 1864 and was entirely rebuilt after the war in 1871. As you can see it's made entirely of brick and stone. Some think it might have been an outdoor kitchen, which would explain why it didn't burn when the rest of the plantation did. But the house, being built into the hill as you see, meant that the cellar was almost untouched by the disaster. The family lived in that space for a time, before taking up residence at nearby Rosedale Manor which you can see through the trees there. Interestingly enough, the cellars were never quite unoccupied though. Confederate soldiers used it as a place to hide when traveling behind enemy lines. That door there leads into the cellars. Someday we'll put a bar there and make this patio an outside dining area, and maybe add a stage for live music. All that's in the future though."

Mrs. Rothschild was waiting for them in the parlor when they finally returned back inside.

If Désirée hadn't spent some time looking up her client online before meeting her today, she might have been caught off guard by the woman who greeted her now. Given the woman's fine attention to detail, you would expect her to be fussy in her appearance. Instead, the woman who greeted her was tall and angular, her long limbs showed off by the simple silk camisole she wore with jeans that rode low on her hips. She moved with a feline grace when she stood up to greet Des, her manicured nails and the diamond studs in her ears her only concession to fashion or wealth. Her skin was light and youthful, and her hair hung in braids which trailed down past her hips.

She spoke with a soft Creole accent as she greeted Des. "I am glad to see you settled in. Did you enjoy the tour?"

Des settled in the indicated chair across from him, noting the way Mr. Quinn had already vanished into one of the many passageways in the house. "Very much."

"I hope you took the time to better understand the challenges which will await you. I have a revised schedule here. Please note the changes..."

For the next hour, Des was bombarded with information, much of which she would have given anything to have in her possession a week ago. No, a month ago. The woman wanted things which couldn't be done, though somehow Des knew she was going to have to make it all happen. It wasn't until Mrs. Rothschild took her leave that she realized to what extent she was going to have to work to pull off the events leading up to the Christmas ball.

She had three days to do a month of prep work.

"I'm doomed," she moaned, flipping through pages of information.

Somewhere in the room an object rolled off a table and smashed.

Dramatic, but appropriate. Especially when Mimi Rothschild showed up.

Mimi proved that the Rothschilds had inherited the genetic lottery. While Mrs. Rothschild had looked to be in her twenties, her daughter...looked almost the same. It was eerie how alike they were in appearance. Mimi though was more into labels and came strutting in wearing a red dress which Des knew she'd seen online for more than she made in a month.

Mimi also came with a double dose of attitude.

She dropped a paper on the table in front of Des without so much as an explanation. "There are the things I'll be needing. Mother said you would see to it."

With that she simply turned and walked out, as if that was the end to it,

Des picked up the list and burst out laughing. A karaoke machine? Disco ball? Good lord, what had she gotten herself into?

***

Three days later, Des found out just how bad this was all going to get.

Mimi had already attacked her once that day for failing to obtain the items on her list. Mrs. Rothschild had then informed her that she needed to be treating Mimi as herself, which really didn't bode well for the rest of her stay at the hotel. In the meantime, she was trying to put up decorations in the smallest ballroom and nothing was staying where she was putting it.

"Are you decking the halls, or am I?" she finally asked when a string of tinsel wound itself around a light fixture so high up she'd need a ladder to get it down.

Stifling a scream, Des grabbed for her phone. "Desperate times..." she murmured as she scrolled through a list of notes she'd compiled in the last few months.

"You can calm down right now or I'm going to put something on you, that I guarantee you won't be liking," she called out to the empty room.

Seeing as how the tinsel was still hanging at least eight feet over her head, Des scowled and tapped the screen of her phone.

Immediately a mystical chant filled the room. At least it did until she managed to turn down the volume control a little.

"C'mon, ghosties, you've got to calm down..." she murmured under her breath as the chant continued. She had no idea if anything was happening but the hair was standing up on the back of her neck so that had to be a good sign.

Or not, considering that the temperature in the room suddenly dropped to where she could see her breath.

In the same instant the lights went out.

Which made it really easy to see when the tablecloth caught fire.

Swearing, Des jumped up, waving her phone around until she found the light switch which illuminated the problem. Though the burning table was doing a pretty good job of that. Swearing up a storm, she grabbed for the fire extinguisher near the door which proved far heavier than she'd expected. Staggering, she tried to aim the nozzle at the blaze.

Only there was no blaze.

Instead, Francois stood on the opposite side of the table, as naturally as if he'd been there all along.

Unfortunately, while her own heart leapt at the sight of him, his expression was so still as to be stern, even angry. "*Cherie*, have you ever considered there are things in this world with which you should not be meddling?" he asked, his voice hard and cold.

Maybe cancelling their date by note, hopefully he at least saw it, may have been more of a blow than she would have guessed.

Chapter 3

Francois

F RANCOIS KNEW SOMETHING WAS wrong, terribly wrong. He could feel it charge the air, he could smell it like ozone after a lighting strike. As he hurried toward the greatest concentration of power, the way the hair on the back of his neck rose up urging him to greater speed.

He dare not blow his cover, not when he'd put so much effort into building this persona. Tearing through the place like a fireman in search of trapped children wasn't really an option. Still, that was what it felt like. The sounds coming from the room ahead made it worse. Dimly he heard some kind of chant, a...spell? Someone was using power and whoever it was sucked at it.

He broke into a run, coming around the corner from the hall and flung himself into a dark room containing among other things, a burning tablecloth and a woman frantically using her phone as a flashlight. The fire was wrong, not acting as a fire should. Which was probably a good thing given a true conflagration would have sent the whole place up in a matter of minutes. For that matter, the woman wasn't exactly right either, something about her was decidedly off. Of the two, the fire was the more immediate concern. It was starting to burn the table underneath.

He reached out and squelched the flames as she found the light switch. There were still a number of threads running through the room, like the ones he'd discovered as a child, and these seemed...angry. He did not have the time to play with energies at the moment and damping the flame had taken more out of him than he wanted to admit. He was likely worthless for a good hour thanks to her. He'd have to rest to regather some of the strength he'd used.

He didn't have time for lying around. He'd had more than he could tolerate of that in recent weeks anyway resulting from a run-in with a giant.

She turned and nearly shrieked. It took every ounce of control for him to school his features and not let his shock at seeing her show. It was the girl. The cute one from the voodoo shop. What in the world had she been playing with to cross the threads like that? This was a deliberate attack and she had to have pissed someone off big time.

Francois always told his friends he had a charmed life, that God himself considered him a favorite son, but seeing her here was the absolute worst thing that could happen. Not now. Not with so much riding on the outcome of the next few days.

Not to mention what she was doing was damned dangerous.

"*Cherie*, have you ever considered there are things in this world with which you should not be meddling?" he asked, his voice hard and cold.

"Well, hello again." She smiled, or tried to, though she seemed more than a bit confused. She looked from the tablecloth – what remained of it – to him and back again. "What are you doing here?"

"What am I..." He sputtered the word. "*Mon cheri*, I appear to be putting out fires. Might I suggest you refrain from restarting another? This establishment burned down once, perhaps we can avoid a repeat."

"Yes…" she seemed flustered, and Francois knew he had to keep her off balance for her safety as well as enabling him to do his job. "I don't know how…"

"Casting spells in an unfamiliar language will carry risks, or did you not understand that?"

"It was…" she looked at her phone, "…YouTube…"

Francois felt his jaw drop. She was invoking power from an online video? "Such things are not the intended purpose of social media. Confine yourself to medical self-diagnosis."

"You don't remember me…" She sounded hurt and Francois nearly broke cover to assure her, but that would have been the most dangerous thing he could have done. The only way to keep her safe was to keep her at a distance. Maybe he could convince her of an evil twin later, or an entire flower shop of apologies, but for now…

"*Mon cheri*, I do not remember you, because I have never once laid eyes on you, and I do not believe that I would care to again. Good day to you." He bowed at the waist and turned on one heel feeling as though he had just kicked a puppy. He paused at the doorway. "Oh. And bless your heart, madam."

He threw that one hoping she would understand that his attitude and speech was an act, that she would leave an opening for him to make it up to her one day, but from her expression, it seemed as though she wasn't reading minds that day.

Great.

He had a jewel thief to catch, a job to do. The fact that he might have just thrown out a chance for happiness, or at least an opportunity to indulge in what would be sure to be a memorable encounter would have to wait. Right now, he needed to get to his room and lie down before he faceplanted somewhere less comfortable.

He was staggering by the time he opened his door, asleep before his body hit the mattress.

It wasn't until he woke hours later that he realized just how deadly of a mess he'd stepped into.

Chapter 4

Désirée

F IVE HOURS LATER AND the room still smelled vaguely of something charred, and the guests arrived.

Désirée stood at the cusp of a dozen gala days of Christmas Wonder wondering why in the world she'd ever thought pivoting into the world of event planning was somehow superior to her previous job in social work. Hadn't she left because there had been too much pressure to do too much with too few resources, the constant stress of never being able to accomplish the things you knew would make a difference?

She flew about adjusting small details, fussing at the waitstaff to make sure they were in place and handling details from the kitchen regarding which appetizers needed to go out first. It seemed if she wasn't everywhere at once, the whole affair would crumble – and this was just the mixer launching the event. She had to forcibly remind herself that she loved this job and was good at it.

Especially with Quinn hovering, as if expecting her to do something terrible to his precious hotel.

Like burn it down?

Désirée winced, not wanting to revisit the memory or the cutting remarks of one very full-of-himself nuisance. It stung that she had initially been delighted by the possibility his arrival had presented only to be dismissed. Was it revenge for the note? It was the kindest thing she could think of at the time. It was not as if she'd asked him to help put out that fire. She'd had the whole thing under control just fine.

"You have this under control, do you not?" Mimi Rothschild appeared at her elbow with a most unsightly sneer marring her pretty face. "Because I could swear we've already run out of my favorite little snacks. Those darling things on the crackers…"

"Are right here," Désirée interrupted, reaching out to intercept a tailcoated server carrying a tray full of delectable savory bites.

Mimi gave her a look and with a toss of her head, took her snacks and departed. Désirée let out a breath she hadn't even realized she'd been holding.

Only three more hours of this and she'd be done for the day, right?

At the moment at least, things seemed to be working out. At least it was if you ignored the way the light in the corner flickered occasionally or the way there were ripples in the punch bowl when no one was standing near it.

Désirée closed her eyes and counted to ten. She reminded herself that old buildings had quirks. The punch bowl rippled because people were walking around creating vibrations in the floor. Old buildings had weird problems with electricity from time to time. Nothing strange was happening. Not like it had been earlier in the small room she'd been preparing for tomorrow's luncheon.

Maybe I should just check on things in there. This seems to be going well enough.

Des let the woman managing the wait staff know where to find her if there were problems and slipped down the hallway toward the small dining room. Here at least things looked under control. The Christmas tree in the corner was on, empty present boxes of varying sizes skirted the tree, lights flickered in a sparkle of white fairy lights which reflected in the mirrors around the room giving the place a magical air. The tables were set with elegant centerpieces setting off each to perfection. She'd been particularly proud of the centerpieces, each of the tiny replicas of the large Christmas tree were decorated with sparkling pairs of earrings which hung like ornaments. At the end of the ladies' luncheon, each woman in attendance would be invited to find a pair of earrings she liked from her table to take as a gift.

Des smiled as she gazed around, feeling peace steal over her.

Until she saw the figure standing in the shadows on the other side of the room.

Francois?

Wary, she strode across the room, half-ready for a confrontation.

"Now, I know you're not in here to mess up my pretty decorations," she said as she joined him in staring at the large tree. She's spent hours making sure every ornament was very precisely where she wanted it.

"You wound me, *ma chere*. I was only admiring. I have never seen so many diamonds in one place."

Désirée could feel some of the tension draining out of her shoulders. "I wanted to carry the motif for the centerpieces over to here. It is something, isn't it?"

It had taken her ages to find the ropes of rhinestones she'd used as garlands, the silver and gold filigree ornaments, the shining baubles. She'd meant for the tree to give the appearance of a jewelry box overflowing. "I honestly worried that it was too much."

"For Christmas? It is not possible. Christmas is all about enjoying life to the fullest. To making a gift of every moment." His expression grew troubled. "Which is why I think you need to leave this place. Quickly. Before the holiday arrives."

"Now wait just a minute..."

"You do not understand what you are dealing with…"

Dealing with? Like the falling ornaments, the ways doors blew shut when there was no breeze? The inn was decidedly haunted, and she might have made some mistakes with trying to combat the problem using the internet as a guide, that didn't mean she wasn't perfectly capable of *dealing* with it.

"No. I mean just that. No. This is my chance and you're not going to scare me out of here just because you think you know more about the supernatural. I mean sure, you're cute and all and you know your way around a voodoo shop but that doesn't make you an expert on whatever this…" she waved her arm to indicate the entire inn, "…is."

"What Voodoo shop, *Cheri*?"

Weirdly enough, he was starting to smile, which stopped her from arguing with him. It wasn't the reaction she expected. Nor did she think he would grab her suddenly and drag her halfway across the room.

"What are you doing? Release me you—"

His hand covered her mouth, cutting off a stream of imprecations. She fought then fiercely instead, though it wasn't anywhere near as satisfying, though the moment her shoe connected with his shin gave her at least some satisfaction.

She struggled. She writhed. She tried desperately to get away…kind of. Somehow this contact brought her into the circle of his arms, and being there didn't feel quite so bad as she'd expected. In fact, she was rather enjoying the confinement, the way her body fit against his, the warm strength of his arms. Francois was one very fit man.

She might have wriggled into a better position, her head tilting up to taste those lips because suddenly she had to know how he tasted even if he'd been blowing hot and cold at her ever since she'd met him.

He shoved her behind him with a muttered, "Stop it, I beg of you my sweet. LOOK."

The door opposite them had opened. A shadowy figure slid into the room as if trying to become one with the darkness. Désirée gasped when she saw this individual go straight for the Christmas tree and do something to the branches.

Who was messing with her holiday decorations?

She started forward, ready to do battle if necessary, but a hand on her arm stopped her. Francois had carried her halfway across the room, and right now they were standing in the shadows. For the moment, they were unseen. Was she really going to spoil that to give someone a dressing down when maybe it would be better to wait and see what they were up to?

Because something here was clearly afoot, and the handsome stranger who had yanked her out of sight had some stake in this.

Désirée wasn't entirely sure she liked mysteries interfering with her chance to make it big.

She stepped forward anyway, but he didn't let go of her.

The figure at the tree was straightening. The enormous hoodie made it impossible to see a face, or guess at the gender of the figure, especially coupled with baggy jeans a couple sizes too large.

The stranger turned to go. Whoever it was should have been looking right at them.

Yet it was clear that somehow his or her gaze saw nothing. Des went so far as to wave her hand when they had to be staring right at her, and they did not react. There was no sign the stranger had seen her at all.

In fact, they quite simply turned and left.

The moment the door shut, Des was all over Francois.

"What was that all about?" she asked, spinning around to face him. She was startled by the grey tinge to his skin, the hollows forming in his cheekbones, the lines settling around his eyes and mouth.

He was aging right before her eyes.

She recoiled from him, struggling to know what to even ask him as he strode past her to the tree.

"Tell me what does not belong here," he said, his crisp words an order even if there was a rasp to his voice which wasn't there a moment ago.

She hurried after him. "I don't know. I didn't memorize every ornament."

Well, she kind of had. This tree had a theme after all.

She started hunting through the branches. "They were standing about here, weren't they?"

"Got it." His breath was still coming in short gasps as he plucked a dark object from the tree. It was one of the voodoo dolls made of twigs and twine she'd seen in the shop where she'd met Francois. "Now what about this screams 'Merry Christmas' to you?" he asked though his grin was shaky. Nor was he as cocky as before.

She reached out to take the object from him but when her skin came into contact with it, there was a distinct sizzle. An electric charge arced over her fingertips and scorched her palm.

The ornament fell to the floor between them. Des, cradling her wounded hand against her stomach, stared wide-eyed at the object, blinking back sudden tears.

Chapter 5

Francois

F RANCOIS FIRMLY TOLD HIS stomach to stay where it was. Folding the threads enough to hide behind was something he didn't like to do because of the nausea and exhaustion involved. As a child, he would trade waking hours for a moment of invisibility if it got him out of trouble. Weaving enough for two to hide behind was ironically more than twice the effort.

The result was slightly less than optimal. He was able to see the...man? woman? plant the charm, but the figure was too well covered to understand who or what it was. Most likely, they had bundled up against the possibility of security cameras, but it was still effective.

Finding the "doll" in the tree was like finding a wine stain on a white jacket. Once you knew to look for it, it stuck out, almost cancerous on the bright tree. On any other tree, it might have blended well with the branches or some trinket a child had made years before and been easily overlooked. In fact, there was a glamour on it that made it difficult to detect, as though the eye wanted to slide off of it.

He pulled it from the tree, though his body protested. His arms and legs wanted to collapse as though the threads had weight and he'd been shoring them up on his own muscle and bone. But there was a job to do first. In this case it was more akin to weapon disposal.

This seemed the day and place for people to call upon powers they didn't understand and couldn't hope to control. It was bad enough the cute girl was playing a YouTube chant, like a DIY spell jukebox, but now this. That little doll had enough thread wrapped around it to be frightening, but it was sloppy. There was a difference between being rushed and not understanding what you were dealing with. This thing seemed to fall into the latter category.

He looked at the tangle of thread woven into the doll, but it too defied even his sight. It was a tangled black mass, a snarl of power. There was no untying that, it had to be snipped and tossed.

He handed it to her as proof of what they had seen. For her...for anyone, it was nothing more than a tangle of twigs and pine needles and a scrap of cloth. It was tied into a roughly man-shaped doll with some old twine. When she took the thing from him, she cried out and dropped it.

Incredibly, it had hurt her. He took her hand in his and examined the wound. It had burned her as if it were steeped in acid like a chemical burn. But looking deeper, he could see the dying embers of thread like filaments in a bulb winding into her palm. That should not have happened.

"*Mon dieu*!" He tried to raise her hand to get a closer look at what had happened, but she avoided his touch, backing away with her eyes wide still staring at the tree.

"It was supposed to be something pretty...to match the fancy diamond they're auctioning for charity on the last night..."

She was in shock, and she needed his help. Francois was beginning to wonder if it was he that was in over his head. Neither the girl with her burning table nor the reaction of the doll on her skin were within the threads he'd known his entire life. *Something here was happening that was powerful and inherently wrong.*

She watched him warily, holding her hand close against her body. "Just what exactly is going on here?"

From her expression and body language, he wasn't going to be able to put off her questions. She had a right to know as well, considering what had happened to her already. Unfortunately, this was not the time or the place, and he could feel the numbness from his exertions taking over his body. He was going to fall.

"*Cheri...*" He began, but his voice was rough and thick. She had already stepped back from him, her eyes wide at his appearance. He didn't want her to be frightened of him, certainly not *for* him, but all he could think of was using that to his advantage. It would buy him time to recover. He cleared his throat and tried again. "I owe you an explanation. *Je suis désolé. Mais maintenant...*" He stopped himself and started over, "at the moment, I am not able to provide the wind to give the explanation you desire. Please, bear with me, allow me some time to regain my strength and I will be delighted to explain everything. Tonight. We will meet in the bar. In the meantime, the best thing for you is to leave, but I already know you will refuse." He held up a hand and graced her with a wan smile. "Avoid as much as you can. Stay safe."

In the meantime, the figure in the hoodie might still be located. The garment was too warm and too...ordinary for the setting. If he could force himself to continue a little longer, he might be able to catch up, or at least determine where the person went. It was pushing himself hard, but that was what he was here for, this was the job description.

But there was still the way she held her palm against her hip. The burn was hurting her and her job required the used of that hand. "Please, if you would just let me see before I go..."

Desiree nodded once and he was able to take her hand in his, palm up and reached for the threads that sat smoldering in her skin. He wove them out, leaving fresh, unharmed flesh behind, and, because he could, he sealed the healed wound with a kiss in the middle of her palm.

He shot her the best smile he could, hoping he didn't look too terribly much like some kind of grinning maniac and hurried from the room. He had to move quickly to catch the thief in the hoodie, but also because he didn't trust his legs to hold him much longer. She'd already been through enough.

He made it out of the door and sagged against the wall while he thought, his hand coming down on a small table. The hallway seemed to stretch out forever, growing longer as he staggered on like something from a fever-induced nightmare. He forced himself upright and took a deep breath.

When the blow to the back of his head erased the light and plunged him into darkness, his body welcomed the rest. He didn't remember hitting the floor, nor did he remember anything after that until he woke.

***

In the course of his life, he had many times been awakened to water being poured or splashed on his face. For a moment, he thought it was happening again, until he tried to gasp and found that instead of water being thrown on him, he had been thrown in water. He was able to get one breath, one sweet, wonderful gasp of air into his lungs before he sank below the surface. Something was pulling him down, inexorably, fatally down.

Whatever it was had hold of his right leg. He kicked at it, but his foot would do nothing but go down. He couldn't get away. His brain wanted to panic. It would all be alright if he could only breathe once more. He just needed air. He fought the terror and felt whatever it was taking him down stop. It was abrupt, as though the creature had hit a wall. Not a wall. The bottom of the pond. Then it wasn't a creature. It was a weight, and what he felt against his ankle was rope or twine...he had been tied to a block and dumped in the pond with his hands tied behind his back. He closed his eyes and reached out with other means.

The threads of the rope and the block itself stuck out like they were neon when he used his second sight to try and see them. By focusing, he could trace each thread. While his lungs burned from lack of air, he pulled, gently, then harder. He could feel the rope around his arms slip free and then his ankle began to move.

He fought against the need to breathe, forcing himself to concentrate on the threads, promising his body fresh, clean air if it could hold out a little longer. He arms free now, he pointed his hands up to the surface and could feel the air on his fingertips.

With a final, almost gentle sigh, the rope around his ankle fell away and he felt himself start to rise. No longer willing to be denied, his body took over. The animal instinct for survival overcoming rationality and calculation.

He clawed his way to the surface and breached like a whale, gasping for the next moment of life, the next clean breath. The pond was deep, but narrow and with some effort he was able to swim and then crawl to the shore where his body fell. He lay coughing up the water he'd accidently consumed already and was able only to arch his back enough to vomit before staggering to his feet.

He was standing behind the plantation, near a carefully cultivated pond. The water was brackish and filled with lily pads and from the sound of it, a fair quantity of frogs. There were few insects around him, places like this would spray for mosquitoes and gnats for the comfort of their guests. Meaning he had just been swimming in insecticide.

"Son of a bitch." He swore as he sat heavily on the ground at the pond's edge. "You *ruined* my suit!"

Worse, from the look of things he'd been out for a while. Judging from how dark it had gotten, he was about to miss his date with Désirée.

Chapter 6

Désirée

D ES HAD ALMOST GIVEN up on Francois. The bartender certainly had. The last drink he'd served her was on the house and came with a look of sympathy and a suggestion that if she was looking for company, he'd be off in an hour.

In fact, she was gathering up her purse and about to go when she saw him come through the door.

Everyone saw him come through the door.

Francois was nothing if not distinctive. He carried himself with confidence, he moved with the grace of a tiger. His suit was designer, and he wore it well.

The fact that he squelched with each step, leaving a trail of water and mud in his wake was especially notable.

Des flew across the room to his side, grabbing at his hands and was appalled when she found them cold and raw. Her fingers came away bloodied.

Why was no one murmuring? Running to assist? Where were the people who worked here? Surely someone would come to assist one of their most distinguished guests? She looked around wildly, realizing that no one was even looking in her direction. It was as if they were not there at all. Even the bartender was looking past her, as if wondering where she had gone.

That thing…whatever he'd done by the Christmas tree earlier. He was doing it again. He was also wavering on his feet, murmuring something she couldn't make out. As if he wasn't even aware she was there.

"Let's get you somewhere you can warm up," she said, and pushed him back the way he'd come. In the hallway, she managed to get his arm slung over her shoulders, using her arm around his waist to guide him in the direction she needed. It occurred to her she had no idea which room was his.

"Don't get any ideas," she told him as she staggered under his weight, thankful her room wasn't far. "I'll have you know I've studied martial arts and can kick your ass from here to next Tuesday if you so much as breathe on me wrong."

He moaned something. It sounded French. Dang but his accent sent fire through her veins.

"Fine, breathe however you like. Only you can let go of that…whatever you do to make us invisible. No one is out here."

At least it didn't feel like anyone was in the hall with them. She was starting to wonder at this place, at how many creatures roamed the halls unseen. Maybe she was speaking too soon. No matter, because they were there already. She propped him against the door so she could get her key card out. He grinned at her blearily and she saw for the first time the growing bruise on his cheek.

"Tell me you at least won," she said shaking her head.

"I'm here, aren't I, *ma belle fille*?"

"That's debatable." The light on the lock clicked green on the fourth try and she was able to shove the door open, and him with it.

He fell into the room before she could catch him, landing on the plush carpet in a heap.

"You are lucky they furnish the rooms so nice. A tile floor would have hurt so bad." She kicked the door shut and dropped to her knees behind him. "My handsome fellow, you need to answer a few things for me if you think I'm going to help you."

He groaned and half rolled over, one palm connecting with the floor so he could leverage himself to a sitting position. "It would be quicker if you were to go home now like I said you should," he growled, and stared at his hand which he was flexing by splaying out the fingers then fisting them. "I think I dislocated my thumb."

"That is what you are concentrating on?" She scrambled up and went to the bathroom to fetch him a towel. "You stink like…"

"Pond water? Insecticide?" He took the towel and mopped at his face. "Did my nose come off when I rubbed my face just now? It feels like my nose came off."

"You were in the pond?"

He was busy pressing his fingers against the end of his nose. "I can't feel that. I don't think it should be numb."

"Francois! What happened?"

"I needed a swim."

"You need an ally."

His head came up sharp. "Not you."

Désirée drew herself up. "What do you mean not me? I'll have you know I live in New Orleans, and I've seen shit. I've even been studying voodoo lore and know enough to recognize a charm with a hex on it when I see one. You think I didn't know right away what I was dealing with when that doll burned me? My family is Haitian for God's sake!"

Francois somehow managed to get to his feet, though he was still wavering. "I don't know what you're talking about. What burn?"

She stared at him. "You know precisely what burn. Why, on this hand here!" She thrust out her palm for him to examine.

"*Cherie*, I see no burn." He placed a kiss there, a twin to the one he'd gifted her with earlier. "It is a rather pretty hand though."

"No." She drew back sharply. "You're not going to do that. I know when someone is trying to gaslight me and it's not sexy or romantic. I'm done with you if you think you're going to make me think something is my fault or that I'm imagining the whole thing."

In that instant a picture fell from the wall, falling behind the TV set with a bang.

They both stared at it. Désirée with a sigh of resignation. Him with a look more inscrutable, more aware than he'd been since she'd dragged him in here.

"I suppose you're going to say I imagined that too," she muttered in disgust and turned away. "I need to get the mud off me. I have no idea how you're managing to wear so much of the bottom of the pond when I assume you had to travel through quite a bit of the watery part on top to get out. You'd think you would you have rinsed off better."

"Madam, it was the mud on the bank which I couldn't avoid."

"Right. You came out of the back side of the pond." She noticed his stare. "There was a little stone jetty which you could have climbed out on, stairs that led right up out of the water...never mind. I noticed it on the tour. My point is we need to get you out of those clothes—"

The look he gave her was pure sex. "Normally I am not one who follows where my partner leads, but I could be willing to see where this goes..."

Des raised one eyebrow, practically daring him to continue that line of conversation.

He didn't.

"As I was saying, you need to get into a shower and clean clothes. Preferably in your own room since I don't think you're my size. Not that I don't think you could pull off the navy pantsuit I've laid out for tomorrow, but it might be snug across the shoulders and other places."

"Agreed. I will be on my way as soon as I..." He seemed to look up then, shaking his head a moment later. "Or maybe not." He winced as he took a cautious step toward her, nearly toppling over in the attempt. "I seem to be a trifle unsteady and the threads in this room are too tangled to draw from."

"Threads?"

He waved off her question. "Never mind...It is..."

She knew what he was going to say because he'd been saying it since they met. "Complicated, yes. Since when has my life since meeting you been anything but...never mind. Let me guess, you need a hand in getting to your room..."

"It is a short way."

"And you can't stay here because..." She gestured toward the loveseat which took up most of the sitting room, because no way was she going to give up her bed in the room beyond. "There is a couch."

"That is not a couch."

No, it really wasn't, and he was quite tall. "Right. Your room. Just...don't bleed on me. Or get more mud on me. I think this suit is probably already ruined but if we could perhaps try..."

"*Oui*, I will do my best," he said and took another step, this one toward the door, only his leg buckled. She only just caught him.

"So, what you're saying is I'm going to be doing all the work?"

"Sadly, this time, yes."

Des pinched the bridge of her nose, trying to stave off the beginnings of what promised to be a nasty headache. "Right. Just tell me which room you're in."

He made a face. "I do not think you will like that answer."

"Try me."

He told her.

He was right. She didn't like it one bit.

Chapter 7

Francois

THE SHOWER HELPED. UNFORTUNATELY, it also helped him feel every bruise and cut that much clearer. He looked at his suit crumpled on the floor. The jacket she had hung on the bathroom door and shoes she had whisked away, but the pants and the shirt he'd been wearing looked lost and forlorn – and absolutely beyond redemption.

He didn't even want to touch it. The hotel had kindly provided bathrobes, and Désirée had made sure that one was accessible before she left him to his own devices. He slipped it on and left the mess where it was.

He hadn't actually expected her to remain while he showered.

She was waiting for him as he exited the bathroom, and his toes grabbed the thick carpeting like a lifeline. She began talking and stumbled over her words and Francois realized that he hadn't tightened the belt on the robe. The important bits were covered, but most of his chest and stomach was not. The robe came together again just where his stomach flattened into the upper part of his hips.

It was far too late to pretend to be modest now, he'd already shown her as much...more than he'd intended, so there was little enough to do but smile. Her flushed cheeks took on a deeper hue. She stared and stopped at the mark on his chest. "Wait...how old is that?"

He looked down, forgetting the nasty scar across his chest. It had healed long enough ago although it was recent enough to look a bit angry against his skin. There was still a faint raised line traced where the wound used to be. "That? That is nothing. It is a reminder of a misspent youth." He gingerly touched the back of his head. "This however, is somewhat more pressing. I washed my hair, but that was quite tender." He turned and bent over slightly for her to inspect the area he was hit.

"I can't tell a thing. Sit down where I can reach you." She snapped and pointed to the edge of the bed. He straightened the robe to be somewhat less revealing and did as she bid. He could feel her sit beside him and gently move the hair out of the way. He winced once when her fingernail hit the exact spot that had laid him out. "If you got knocked out, that's a concussion – by definition. You need to get it checked."

"Ah, *non*. I simply wish to know if I am bleeding, yes?"

"No. I mean...no, you're not bleeding, but you still need to..."

"...have my head examined. *Oui*, I know. I have been told so many times."

"So..." He turned back to face her, waiting for the rest of the sentence. "...fix it."

His expression must have given him away. She cocked her head and waggled her fingers at him. "You know. Voodoo heal it? I mean...remember where we met? I have this...friend who's going through some...stuff and I was there in that shop doing research, trying to understand. I mean I'd never heard of using it for healing, but if you can do it, do it." She held up her hand to show the palm that was perfectly healed.

Francois sighed. He couldn't talk his way out of this one and what was more, she deserved the truth. "It is not as easy as it looks, *cheri*. There is a cost for using the thread and to be very candid, I have been paying for too much use already. The price would be greater than the benefit."

"It cost you to heal me?"

"Oh..." he waved that away. "Compared to the other things I have done today, that was minor enough. Not being seen takes energy...and a few other things I have had to do this day." He felt himself relax, and he let his tongue run a little freer for it. "Worse beat down I ever had, from a giant, no less, I couldn't 'heal' either, it would have been a longer recovery than just lying in the hospital a week."

"Fine." She seemed to suddenly realize she was on his bed next to him. and he was lightly dressed at best. She shifted away, not subtle in her attention...or interest. He hid a smile. That she was bothered gave him hope. She'd been 'bothering' him in the same way since he met her. He considered placing his hand around her thick thigh, but he knew she would skitter away. He liked her to be at ease with him, almost as much as he enjoyed following the trail of his imagination.

"Then what do you need?" She asked, breaking into his ruminations.

He thought for a moment and a thousand flippant answers ran through his head. Somewhere between crude and clever, but she was asking in earnest, and she was trying to help. He shrugged. "Rest. Food. Mostly food."

"Alright, food and rest are my strengths. Let me take care of the details. I can have room service here in an hour, and I will wake you when they get here. I can only assume they come all the way to the caretaker cottage." She shook her head, "You know there are closer rooms."

He grinned. "Aye, but the cottage is a stand-alone and easier to set the threads against intruders." He stood up to follow her out, to get the door for her.

"What do you mean by threads? You've said that several times now."

He opened his mouth to answer. Or to not answer as the case may be, but he couldn't come up with a reasonable sounding explanation fast enough because she put up a hand to stop him.

"On second thought, don't. Not tonight. Right now, you need rest. Maybe some…" she gave him a frank look up and down that left *him* blushing, "pajamas if you have them? I'll manage the rest. Shoo…" She shoved him toward the bed. "Get some sleep."

***

An hour later Francois came awake suddenly, not entirely sure where he was. It took him a minute to place the sound of voices, the sudden smell of steak and garlic mashed potatoes. Dinner had arrived and he hadn't even remembered falling asleep.

She'd ordered a small meal for herself, to "keep him company," but ordered him heavy starches and meat and cheese. It wasn't his usual fare, but he had to admit that it seemed to buoy him better than anything else he'd eaten recently.

"Tell me about this friend," Francois prompted between bites, "the one who is going through some things that made you do research in a voodoo shop."

"I wish I could. You might be able to help." Des leaned back in her chair, eyes distant while she considered the matter. "She doesn't tell me much of what's going on. If you ask me, she's being haunted. I think her dead fiancé has come back but she doesn't say so in so many words. Probably unhappy that she's seeing someone." She paused to pick through her salad, extracting a single slice of cucumber from the rest and eating it. "The problem is, I never much liked the old fiancé when he was alive, and she knows it. I think that keeps her from feeling like she can talk to me about it."

Then she asked about the threads.

He didn't want to answer, but was out of excuses. The food had hit his blood and with the nap he felt himself again, though he would need more sleep before he was genuinely whole. He sighed, knowing he owed her this much. "It started with a dog..."

He spoke of his pet and the way the mysterious woman pulled the threads and healed the animal as it lay dying. He tried to explain what the threads were like, but there was no common reference point he could give. "To be honest, I've never met anyone who does what I do," he said finally. "I wish like crazy I knew who that woman was just so I could ask her about what she did that day."

"So...this thread ability you have...is that why someone tried to kill you?"

Francois thought a moment. "I honestly do not know. I was hired to find a thief, specifically to stop a thief from stealing."

Des gasped. "The Rothschild Diamond."

"*Mais oui*. My employer has reason to believe that an attempt will be made on the jewel at some point before the auction."

"Then why aren't you guarding it?"

"I am." He waggled his fingers at her. "I have enough threads on it to make a rug. I have set traps."

"Seems to me like someone else is setting traps for you and they're better at it." She mimicked hitting his head and despite himself, he flinched before finally laughing.

"Perhaps you are right. At least in part. Sometimes I forget to look at what's right in front of me." He stared at her meaningfully, but she turned away instead of holding his gaze.

"Or right behind as the case may be?"

He needed a good laugh. In fact, she was good for him in general. He was still exhausted, but he had never recovered so fast. "*Merci*," he said softly, "it is good to have someone to talk to about these things. I do not often have that chance."

She ducked her head, but did not look away this time. For a moment, she was there, her eyes locked on his and within reach...desirably, wonderfully within reach.

Until she stood and began stacking the dishes on the little desk where they'd been eating. "I sent your suit to be cleaned. I don't know if they can save it, but it gets it out of the room. It was beginning to smell like my grandmother's old dish sponge." She wouldn't look at him now, but her hands were shaking as she put the dishes to one side.

He stood, but did not approach her. She spoke to the far wall. "I need to go before...before I get in too deep here. I'm..." she turned to him then and looked up at him as if hoping he had the words she couldn't find.

"I am too, *mon cheri*. More than I can tell you. But I beg you... if you will not leave for my sake or yours, please...be very careful. There are dangers here you cannot know."

Des opened the door, and he followed her to the front steps. "I'm a big girl, I can handle myself, but...no, I won't take any unnecessary risks." Her hand fluttered out as though she was going to touch him, reassurance? Attraction? Desire?

Her hand found no purchase and she turned to step off the little porch.

A blood-curdling scream erupted from the main house.

Chapter 8

Désirée

THE NEXT MORNING, DÉSIRÉE was out of sorts as she fussed over last minute preparations. The shopping tour of Baton Rouge was coming together, as was the Christmas Chorale which would be that evening, but there were still last-minute details to attend to. It didn't help that everyone was on edge after last night's disaster.

"I'm telling you Kendis, for a while there my heart was in my throat. When they said some piece of jewelry was stolen, my first thought was that the blasted diamond had disappeared. Thankfully it was only a bracelet, some piece more sentimental than valuable, but it's still disturbing." Désirée stood back and studied the chair arrangement for the concert and nodded to herself that the small ballroom looked perfect.

"Does that affect your preparations?" Kendis asked, her voice sounding faint through the Bluetooth headset Des wore.

"Not much. I'm still here doing my thing while there's added security. They have some plainclothes officers doing a walkthrough of the public areas a little more often. We'll also have an extra couple of guards on the diamond at the auction the night of the ball." She shuddered. "Still puts me on edge. There's a lot of funny stuff going on…"

"Funny stuff...?"

Des had hesitated to bring it up, but for a while now she'd been playing this cat and mouse game conversationally with her best friend where they both didn't quite talk about the weird supernatural stuff going on around her and Jason. Much as she wanted answers, was this really the time? Besides it would only lead to questions about Francois, and she wasn't sure she was ready to talk about the flirty Cajun in her life just yet.

"Nothing. In fact...I think someone wants me. Gotta go." Des disconnected as a small contingency came into the room, led by Mrs. Rothschild and Mr. Quentin who, despite the Santa hat he wore, looked anything but festive. Especially in the way he had a laptop tucked under his arm.

The group came and stood in front of her, then seemed confused by who was the spokesperson, with Mrs. Rothschild and Mr. Quentin both starting at the same time.

"Miss..."

"Do you mean to tell me..."

They stopped and looked at each other while Des crossed her arms, not liking where any of this was going. She knew the routine. She was a new business owner, the low man on the totem pole who had gotten this job because of a connection who had recommended her despite the fact she was just starting out.

She was about to be blamed for something and wasn't about to have any of that. Not when she knew beyond a shadow of a doubt what she was going to be blamed for likely had to do with that damned bracelet, and she had a solid alibi for last night. To her way of thinking, they might as well bring it, if they were so intent on making fools of her.

So, she waited them out while they sorted the hierarchy. It was Mrs. Rothschild who spoke first.

"What do you know about this man?" she asked, and gestured to Mr. Quentin who was already opening up the laptop to show a grainy image of Francois creeping through the hotel.

Francois, who looked very much like he did right now, appeared in the doorway somewhat flustered, but in a fine suit and carrying with him an aura equal parts confusion and anger.

Oh, she didn't need this, nor did she need them seeing him, so she spoke loudly, "I know very little about anything other than the work I've been doing here. Or that I'm trying to do right now to make sure the next event goes off without a hitch. Unless you're interested in doing the lighting checks with me, Mrs. Rothschild. I'm sure you won't mind standing in the spotlight while I set things up."

With that she brushed past them all, stepping past them so she could give Francois a violent shake of the head, mouthing for him to beat it before someone turned and saw him.

Only he wasn't listening and apparently her adversaries had a lot more to say on the subject than she'd expected.

Mrs. Rothschild followed her around to where she was checking cords for the can lights. "I'm trying to talk to you about this man who you were seen with last night. We have reason to believe he's a jewel thief."

"I was seen with!" She started to laugh except the image on the laptop had changed to the one where she was walking down the hallway with her arms around Francois, trying to get him into her room.

Oh. My. Goodness.

"Well, if you know I was with him, I don't know what you're asking about. What my boyfriend and I do when I'm off the clock is hardly the concern of—"

The image changed again. Francois in the same suit was picking the lock of another door in the hallway and letting himself into the room. He came out a moment later, something bright and shiny in his hand which caught the light, so the stones glittered.

Well, that was just stupid. What jewel thief walked around waving the stolen goods around so any fool could see it? It was so clearly a faked image, it could have been used for stock footage in a Scooby Doo cartoon. She was laughing without meaning to and had to stop to brush tears from her eyes.

"Okay well that's just ridiculous. We went to his room not long after, I'm sure you have footage of that. Then I ordered room service while he...well, never mind what he did. But your time stamps would surely show where we were, when."

Mr. Quentin interrupted here. "Are you implying someone tampered with these images? Because I assure you, they were taken with the same cameras on the same night."

"You might as well confess it," Mrs. Rothschild said. "Clearly you ordered food to cover for your lover while he went out a window in the back of the bungalow and burgled poor Mrs. Hutchens suite, taking her bracelet."

"You think I would risk my career on a pretty bauble when there's a ginormous Christmas ball in a few days where a diamond as big as my head is being auctioned? You have to hear how ridiculous that all sounds...."

"*Cherie*..." Francois had somehow joined them without any of them noticing. That Désirée jumped as his hand slid around her waist hopefully went unnoticed. Then, he gently caressed the small of her back, both calming and exciting her. While the touches were not inappropriate under the circumstances, they triggered dirty thoughts and promised tingles in places she could not afford to think of in this moment. She gave him a sharp look, but he only raised a hand to smooth a strand of hair back behind her ear, all the while holding her gaze with a look so intense it was a wonder she didn't melt on the spot. "My sweet, I can speak for myself, though I admire your defense of my character." He turned toward the others, "Search my room. Search myself if you need to. You will not find any pretty baubles. I am here to celebrate the holiday with the one I love, stolen moments when she is not busy. Surely you understand I would not waste a precious second of our time together by chasing after party favors I have no need of."

His husky voice, the velvet smoothness of his speech left Des gaping for longer than perhaps was necessary but for a moment she was caught up in the fantasy of what it might be like if these words had been spoken in earnest.

Hell, she wanted those words to be spoken in earnest. Her legs were about to give out, especially when he tugged her against him, his arm going naturally about her waist. "Come my love, we can monitor their search from the sanctuary of the lover's embrace..."

"Now see here, this is quite unorthodox!" Mr. Quinn blustered, but Mrs. Rothschild only shook her head.

"I say we do it. We search the rooms, right now. I, in fact, insist upon it. Their cars too. Heaven knows where they might have hidden..."

"But we would need a warrant..." Quinn said with an uneasy look at Francois who waved.

"Francois, what if someone planted it..." Des whispered, pressing closer to him in a way which wasn't exactly pretense anymore. Oh, it was nice to feel the strength in his forearm against the small of her back.

"I am sure they have. But they will not find it." A bead of sweat appeared on his forehead though he made no move to wipe it away. "Which is why you need to leave."

"If I go now my reputation will be ruined and I will lose everything. My business..."

"Your business or your life, *ma chere.* You saw last night they have no qualms in doing murder. And the ghosts in the employ of the thief are using one of the most dangerous of creatures..."

"Creatures?"

"The doppelganger. One who is quite skilled at taking the face of another." He brushed his lips against her ear in a show of tenderness which hid a most urgent whisper. "Trust no one if you stay...not even me."

Mr. Quinn turned toward them suddenly. "Security will search your rooms," Mr. Quinn finally decided, and Francois bowed.

"And I will watch to make sure none of your staff attempts to place within my belongings something which does not belong. I suggest you do the same, my lover."

"Yes...Yes of course." Désirée said immediately, and gave Mrs. Rothschild a look. "As soon as we clear up whether I am still in the employ of Mrs. Rothschild.

"Well, of course..." Mrs. Rothschild shifted uncomfortably. "I would not...I mean...It is he who is the problem..."

"Then let us get this over with because the musicians will be setting up shortly and I will need to run sound checks with them, as well as manage a dozen other details before your guests return from their shopping excursion. Unless you would like to handle these things?"

The look she got from Mrs. Rothschild answered that.

"Then let's get on with this. I don't have all day." Des shot a look at Francois, stepping regretfully from his arms. Despite his advice to not trust him or anyone else, she hated leaving him behind, especially when it had felt so natural to be in his arms.

She really did have the worst timing sometimes, and around him, always.

Chapter 9

Francois

T HE SUIT HAD BEEN restored well enough. The hotel cleaners
had to have despaired at the condition. But by some miracle of
dry cleaning, he was able to wear it again. In fact, he wore it as he joined
her at the table. She was tearing apart the sandwich as though it had
offended her.

"*Bon jour.*" He swung one leg over the chair and settled beside her.

She set the sandwich down and looked at the even pieces. "I really
hate being accused of...of..."

"Is it theft or infidelity you chafe at? For my part, I have many times
been falsely accused of a great deal of mischief, but I rather find myself
enjoying the thought of you and I being together. I cannot deny a
certain joy in this."

She lifted her glass of water and held it a moment before drinking.
"Problem is, I'm supposed to be a professional. For that matter, my
business is on the line here, or at least my reputation. Until we can
clear your name, mine isn't going to be worth much."

"I am sorry that you have found yourself in such an untenable
position. As there is no evidence of any wrongdoing, save a grainy
image of some version of myself flagrantly displaying the trinket, there
was no reason to harass us further."

He started as a long, drawn-out note sounded behind him. Des shrugged apologetically, "I have to be here for the orchestra to warm up." As he watched, more musicians filtered in choosing chairs and instrument stands.

"This is really quite the production." He watched as they took their places.

"And I'm coordinating the entire thing. Which in this case, is very much like trying to herd cats. Feral cats." She took a torn piece of sandwich. "But this is why I am putting up with false accusations and searches. This is the biggest job my fledgling company ever had and if I drop the ball on this, there won't be another chance."

She paused as a waiter came and set a plate with a sandwich on it in front of Francois. "This is what the staff is getting while they prepare the real food. I didn't have time to make something more...elegant, but I remembered what you said about food helping you out."

He lifted the sandwich and took a bite, it was a simple turkey sandwich, but it was unexpectedly good. The meat was tender and there was a hint of dill added to the mayonnaise that made the ordinary have a slight tang he found enjoyable. "*Merci*. It is *tres bon*."

"Besides," Des continued he ate, "someone has to help you guard the 'treasure'." She waggled her fingers as though providing visual effects to her words and he tried to contain his laughter until after he swallowed.

"I will be happy enough after it is auctioned tomorrow evening and no longer my..." he amended himself quickly, "...*our* problem."

"That is my entire strategy," Des confessed, "get through 'till tomorrow. Once this job done, I will be happy to leave this place behind me. If I flee fast enough, I can spend Christmas in New Orleans with my friends."

Francois looked into her eyes and found himself smiling, not at what she said, but because it was enjoyable to be around her. "Although I too will be happy enough to leave this place and its strange powers, I cannot fault the entire trip. There have been very enjoyable...aspects to this journey we are on. Meeting you has been a truly wonderful happenstance."

"Well..." Des grinned. The smile hit her eyes and the room seemed brighter, "you didn't hear me complain when they thought you and I were..."

"...in love?" Francois pressed the word. It was too soon to make a declaration, but to be mistaken for lovers was not a bad thing. Any man would be proud indeed to have her on his arm and she was proving to be a valuable part of the investigation as well. Beauty, charm and wit.

"Yeah. Well..." She took a drink and watched as the leader of the orchestra called last-minute instructions to his musicians. In a moment, a lyrical tune seemed to still the room, the music taking the edges off the day.

"*Bon.*" The word escaped his lips, he hadn't realized he was going to say anything, but the musicians were good. He was sitting in a high-end restaurant with a beautiful woman as a private orchestra played just for them. He found he could be easily contented with a life as this.

"You should probably get some rest," Des stood, much to his surprise. "We both have a very busy day tomorrow and you need to be able to weave...or sew, or whatever you call what you do."

He looked at the orchestra and then back to her and took another drink of water. "*Mais oui.*" It seemed as though when the conversation began to be intimate, she retreated. He-swallowed the things he wanted to say, the things he probably *shouldn't* say. She hadn't refused him and he wasn't about to give up, but if she needed him to go slowly, well, she was worth the wait.

"And what will you be doing, *mon chéré*?" He stood and waited for her answer.

"I need to go and check on that tree. There was something very off-putting about that ornament appearing there. Like it was a warning. We have not paid enough attention to that detail I think." She had a very determined look to her face. There was no talking her out of it, he could tell. He began to wonder if she'd had a premonition.

"I will come with you and then go to my room after we have ascertained the condition of your tree."

"You put that charming decoration back in the tree?"

"*Mais oui*. Whoever placed it there will never know it was disturbed. Why?"

"Another thought…what if the ornament was not a warning but was instead put there as a message. If that's true, then there's more than one person behind this."

"*Mon dieu.*" Francois swore under his breath. "I have not been thinking clearly. Of course. It would have taken at least two people to have thrown me into the pond between my weight and the weight of the block."

He followed her to the tree which looked undisturbed. A close inspection revealed that the doll was still in place, like a dark blot in the center of the light.

"What is that?" Des knelt and peered between branches behind the doll. "I did not put that there."

There was a new decoration, a silver ball that might have been easily overlooked as it added itself to the general shine of the tree. The ball boasted etchings, symbols that made his skin crawl to look at.

He reached in to carefully pluck it from the branch. Des hissed a warning, but the bobble didn't burn him the way the doll had burned her.

He pulled it out and noted a thin line that ran the circumference of the ball. He took hold of the top and the bottom and twisted.

The ball opened and spilled its contents on the floor at his feet.

"The bracelet," Des whispered.

Chapter 10

Désirée

D ES STARED IN HORROR at the bracelet. "A trap or a test run?" she asked, standing to look quickly around the room to make sure they were still alone.

"I have no idea. *Non*, do not touch it. It might burn you. I must put this away...though if I do, someone might open the ornament and think you are the thief. Bah, what a problem. This I did not sign up for."

"Neither did I," she shot back. "Why are you not getting that out of sight."

"Because someone has learned from their mistakes." He flinched, murmuring something just under his breath as he fished the object up from the tree skirt and somehow managed to scoop it back into the bottom half of the ball.

"It's burning you?" she asked, horrified at the level of concentration it seemed to take him to seal the ball again.

"It is a curse, of that there is no doubt."

"Can you undo it?" She thought she heard voices from the hallway. Panicking, she shifted her body so that if someone came through the door, they would not be able to see what they were doing by the tree.

With any luck, maybe they could be seen to be admiring it. Or, given the way he was kneeling over the bauble, that he was proposing.

Wouldn't that open another kettle of fish though? Just how far would she have to go in her imaginary relationship with Francois to protect herself?

And why was she wishing that it wasn't imaginary, especially when there were more dire matters to focus on?

Oh heavens, the voices were stopping outside the room, and he still hadn't managed to place the top back on the ornament.

"We are out of time," she hissed, and with a quick inhalation of breath to steel herself for whatever came next, she grabbed the bracelet and ornament from his hands and took off running.

All Des could think was how important neither of them were caught with the bracelet. Right now, she had absolutely no explanation for having it in her possession, nor would she be able to explain the searing pain accompanying the act of carrying it. She could only imagine how the flesh looked underneath.

That was no matter now. She needed to hide, quickly. Des was dimly aware of Francois somewhere behind her. That he was trusting her to lead the way spoke volumes. Unfortunately, there was only one place she could think to go.

The doors to the stairs were not kept locked, though there were signs which explained these areas were not for guests. The question was, which door led to the older basement, the one with the tunnels under the house?

Des cast the question out to the universe, "Find it for me." The words became a desperate plea which was meant for...well, whatever had been bothering at her all week. They'd been having their fun at her expense, and she'd even left them to it in some cases. At least she hadn't tried anymore online videos to tame them. To her way of thinking, they owed her.

So, when one of the doors swung open at her approach, she plunged through without questioning it, stumbling on the first step and clattering down far faster than she was comfortable with. Especially since she hadn't so much as taken a moment to turn on the lights.

"Francois?"

She thought he was behind her. Surely, he had to have some way to pierce the darkness which was thick as a blanket. It was like running with her eyes closed, though she knew they were wide open.

She hit the bottom stair, and the floor just beyond came up and startled her, so that she fell forward. She was surprised to find the floor here was dirt, not concrete. Basements were not common here to begin with, and to have it left unsealed seemed to invite disaster. Somehow though, she knew where to go, crawling forward even as a light flashed, illuminating the darkness.

"Francois?" Her voice wavered as she called to him. Her good hand cupped the one holding the ornament, smoke rising from the flesh. She could not let it go yet, though her body bent in agony, tears streaming down her face and ruining her makeup. Désirée was not one to ruin her makeup for no good reason, nor was she of a mind for any man to see her in this state.

It was a point of stupid pride, especially when the shadows around them moved weirdly, and not at all in the way that shadows should.

No. Not shadows. Shadow figures. The long arms and legs arranged themselves into men, many men drawing around them, growing more solid as they assembled.

"FRANCOIS!"

She did look then, wild and needing to see his face. He was there, holding aloft the light, his lips moving as if praying.

No, not praying. Trying to control what was around them. Gathering threads? There had to be too many. She pictured knotted yarn. It would do no good to pull one when it was so bound up with everyone else's.

"You..." She addressed the ghosts, gasping out the words. "You know what it is to hide from an enemy. You answered my call when I begged for a place to go. Now you must show me what to do with this."

She thrust the object toward them with more force than she meant to, flinging it into their midst.

The shadow figures recoiled then drew in around it, bending over the ball and bracelet while Des, no longer able to hold back the scream of pain, which had been building for far too long already, crumpled into a heap, sobbing. Her hand, her hand would never uncurl again, never be able to grip, never be able to do a thousand things she used a hand for. It had been burned, scorched until it was a blackened claw, charred and no longer truly any part of her.

"Can we leave it here?" she asked between sobs. "No one will find it here. Tell me this is enough. Oh Francois, tell me this is enough!"

Chapter 11

Francois

F RANCOIS FELL TO ONE knee, reaching for where he knew her hand to be. In the darkness, he should not have been able to see it at all, but the spirit energy emanating from the wound might as well have been a beacon.

She flinched at his touch and pulled away instinctively. He could not allow her to ignore this though, not when he could see that the burn was bad, much worse than last time. He pulled on his shirt tail and tore a swath to wrap her hand. *"Je suis désolé, mon cher.* I am sorry, but I have not the strength to heal this." He wrapped the torn cloth around the wound. "Keep this on so that it does not get infected."

She winced when he wrapped her hand. Maybe if he couldn't heal her injury, he could still help to numb it, at least a little. He pulled what he could, moving the threads until his body began to shake from the effort.

"Je suis vraiment désolé. I am only sorry you have been caught up in all of this, *mon ange."* He kept talking, trying to distract her from what he was doing. From what was forming around them. His second sight had allowed him to see the creatures in the darkness the moment they'd come into this horrific space. He only prayed she was blind to

them, as lost in the darkness as more mortals would be. "You can still leave this place. I will help you to get to your car…"

Des shook her head, but was still cradling her hand. "No, I will not run—"

"You must!"

"Francois!" She spoke sharply but the look she gave him was tender, her voice softening as she continued. "I'm an adult, allow me to decide this for myself. Besides, right now, our fates are entwined."

How could he argue with such a thing?

Groaning because he was still sore from his own encounters with their enemy, he helped her stand, though he was none too steady himself. As one, they turned their attention to the shining bracelet on the dirt floor. It emanated a ghostly green light, making dirt around it look poisoned, like a wound.

"You see it then," he said softly.

"I would have to be blind not to." Her gaze flickered to the shadow figures around them. "I see all of it."

She caught him by surprise with this admission. That she was so steady in the face of a physical manifestation of the supernatural spoke volumes. "Then you know how evil the spell is which is attached to it." He gave a wry chuckle. "And how important it is that we have a very long talk someday when we are done with this place."

"Francois," Des moved in a slow circle around the piece, wincing when the shadowy figures that had been surrounding them seemed to huddle in closer, also curious. "What can we do to safely dispose of that thing? We have to put it back or…or something. Can we make a plan, or maybe…"

"I can return it." Francois was already thinking about how. "*Mais*, I will need a distraction."

She raised her injured hand as if to remind him that her abilities were sharply curtailed. "What did you have in mind?"

"Perhaps you remember when we met..."

"At the voodoo shop? Yes."

"*Non, mon cher*, where we met here, at this place. The flaming tablecloth."

Des cleared her throat. "I remember."

"Well, there are tablecloths and candles galore upstairs, perhaps you can repeat that spell? It would be an effective distraction to say the least."

"I suppose." She sounded unsure, but Francois suspected that it was the embarrassment of being discovered spell casting that she reacted to. Though the table fire was an unintended consequence of her attempt. "I can always play the thing again."

"*Mon cher*, the words are nothing, they serve only a focus. It is the heart of the spell caster, the need of the moment that determines the magic. You have the power, I have seen it in you. You only need instruction on how to access it."

She looked up sharply, surprised by his words, but said nothing. Francois suddenly sensed something. He broke off and watched as the deep shadows around the room began to coalesce, the dark shapes becoming more solid.

"Francois..." Des grabbed his arm "what is it?"

"I believe the local residents wish to express their opinion on the matter." The shapes became more human, though the features were never plain. They suggested bodies, inferred that there were legs shuffling across the floor. As they moved, they became more distinct, different heights and shapes and some semblance of what they once were, and how they met their end.

Twisted shapes bespoke violent ends, staggering movements spoke of broken bones, of flesh failing before the release of death had taken them. They seemed most interested in the bracelet and the ball with strange markings. They gathered around these as though being summoned and then, when the baubles failed to rise, turned their collective attention on Francois and Des.

"There are…"

"…ghosts." Des filled in. "The dead of this place are gathered here. Only…" she put out a hand to the nearest and only just stopped herself from touching it. "I think they are more solid than ghosts ought to be."

"Not quite manifest," he murmured, liking this situation less and less.

"I think they are attracted to the curse on the ball."

Behind them something rattled.

The banister of the stairs. It moved so far and so fast, it was a wonder it didn't break off into splinters. Des reached with her good hand, grabbing at his arm.

Piles of old junk, left to rot in forgotten darkness shook. The folded legs of card tables clattered like old bones and the shadows came on, each halting step somehow aggressive, hands outreached in claws. Francois did not know if they could hurt them in this state, but the ghosts apparently thought they could.

"We need to leave this place," Francois hissed, his arm going around her, holding her to him.

"Then it is my turn to do something." Des faced the oncoming crowd. "My friend taught me a phrase. Some kind of spell I think." She squared her shoulders and Francois could feel it. The energy in the room shifted, refined and flowed into Des.

It was as though he was suddenly standing next to someone else, something else. The power glowed in her and even in his weakened state, he could see the way the threads wrapped around her. It was primal, beautiful and powerful. In that instant she became a goddess, a devil and an angel and for a moment, the threads around her shone like gold.

She spoke a word. Afterward, he could never remember the word, not precisely, but the power built in her dissipated in a wave. The shadows were simply gone. The room was empty and dark, and the shining baubles simply lay where they had fallen.

"*Mon Dieu*." Francois breathed. "I had not realized..."

"Is..." Des seemed suddenly shy, the goddess had gone and the woman left in her place was very human, though still very lovely. "...is that...okay?"

Francois took her good hand in his, pressing a kiss to her fingertips. "*Tu as bien fait, mon ange.* I do not think I have ever been this turned on by a woman before. Come, let us be away before I express my way in a way which makes us both forget why we are here."

Chapter 12

Désirée

T HE PLAN THEY CAME up with felt too hurried, too cobbled together last minute. Of course, they didn't have a lot of time. The bracelet, at least, was dormant, whatever curse had been laid on it swept bare by whatever Des did.

She was starting to think she should have asked Kendis a whole lot more questions these last months, especially when it was clear she'd been going through something nasty.

I'm going to check in with her when I get home. First thing. In the meantime, we need to settle this. Tomorrow is the auction, and if we don't find the thief and what all this is about, everything falls apart.

Right. Do the stuff.

At least Francois was in possession of the bracelet. The way her hand hurt, the last thing Des wanted was to be anywhere near it, even if it was no longer bespelled. She only needed to dress...

Damn it.

Getting dressed with her hand bandaged, the fingers immobilized like claws...

She was going to be sick if she looked at it. She knew she was. At least, it was mostly numb, thanks to whatever Francois had done to it.

She'd be screaming hysterically otherwise, and on her way to a hospital otherwise.

So long as the effect didn't wear off anytime soon, she'd be okay. In the meantime, she needed something without a lot of zippers to wear tonight. Thankfully she'd packed just the thing.

Wriggling into the sequined material, Des had to admit the gold dress looked amazing on her even if it was a little overdressed for the night's events. The bandage though...she found some long gloves to pair with the dress, stepped into her heels and gave herself a once over. Not bad, even if the makeup had been applied with her 'off' hand.

Trusting that Francois had the security cameras off by now, she left her room, hoping she appeared casual as she drifted through the rooms to be used for tonight's events. She talked to staff, handled last minute questions, and kept a smile on her face somehow even if her hand was starting to ache by the time she made her way back to that small ballroom and the tree there.

A quick glance assured her the room was empty.

Mrs. Rothschild caught up with her outside the room being used for the concert.

"Désirée! I was hoping I'd see you somewhere here. We need to talk."

Des turned with a sinking feeling in the pit of her stomach. No conversation in the history of mankind had ever gone well when starting with that phrase. "Yes, Mrs. Rothschild?"

The woman grabbed her arm and towed her a short distance down the hall. Away from the guests, Des realized. "I need your assurances that there will be no trouble for tomorrow night's ball and the charity auction. We will not have any more incidents, will we?"

Des really was starting to understand why she'd been asked to pull this affair together so last minute. How many others had walked off the job before her? "There will not," she said through gritted teeth, knowing full well there was about to be a disaster which would likely get her fired. "In fact, I was just checking the other rooms being used to make sure the setup for tomorrow was still looking good. You are free to go through these checks with me if you wish."

"I do NOT wish. Though my daughter will be happy to." She motioned to someone behind Des who only just bit back a groan as the younger woman joined them.

Mimi was the last person Des wanted to see. So far, she had only talked to the woman in small doses, but the perpetual sneer and high expectations of the other woman set Désirée's teeth on edge. Still, she was the client, and right now Des needed to make sure she did her part to create a distraction while Francois returned that dratted bracelet.

"By all means. Why don't we check out the dining room for tomorrow's dinner. The tables should be set out by now. We'll start with everyone eating in the space by the jeweled tree and then open up the room the rest of the way for the auction and dancing afterwards...we can't do it now because of tonight's events and the white elephant gift exchange at brunch. Once that's done though, we'll be able to make it all one room again and you'll see how it all looks."

Mimi gave her mother a nasty look as she trailed after Des into the small ballroom. "There's a funny smell in here. Like something..." Mimi gave a hard look at Des. "...burned."

Burned. Heaven help her, but it felt like the other woman knew precisely what she was planning.

No. It was a guess. A trace of smell lingering from the bracelet and the damage it had done to Des's hand which was hurting like crazy now. Much more of this and Des would be in tears.

It had to be now or never.

"Mimi, you said you did not wish to sit with your mother?" she prompted, thinking back to an earlier discussion. "I put you over there by the tree, but now I'm wondering if you'd rather be at the opposite table instead. I placed Eugene Fitzsimmons there. His divorce is final now, isn't it? Can you check the name cards?"

It was a simple ploy to get the young woman away from her while she tweaked place settings and checked the centerpieces, which had been replaced for this event. The small trees were gone, replaced by Christmas flower arrangements with a tall candle in the center of each.

Fake candles. Plastic pillars which you had to turn on to make sure the batteries worked. She went methodically around the room now, turning on each candle, bringing each to life. Ostensibly making sure that each one worked.

Mimi drifted between the two tables with name cards, messing up Désirée's meticulous seating plan along the way.

Perfect. It was perfect for what she was doing.

When she touched the next candle, Désirée murmured a piece of the spell. Different from the one before. Just words Francois had given her to focus her will. All she needed was one of these tables to burn. Just one...a small fire. Something she could try and put out which would explain her burned hand and would draw all the attention on this room so Francois could get rid of that awful bracelet.

Just one flame. All I need is one flame.

She moved to the next table. Chanting softly. Distracted by Mimi and worried. Still chanting. Still trying to focus...

That. There.

She felt it. That strange feeling of tapping into something outside of herself. That...

She pulled at it with her mind, stopping at the table where she first heard the pull. Was this a thread? Was there spectral energy here?

Des started the chant a third time, looking for a wisp of smoke in vain.

Feeling instead a surge of heat behind her.

Désirée shrieked, whirling around in time to see the entire table behind her go up.

It was perfect. No…it was too much. She was going to bring the whole place down.

It doesn't burn the same way a real fire does. It's not true flames. It'll be okay…

All the same, she shouted to Mimi who stood by the door, her mouth agape, staring.

"Mimi, get help! Sound an alarm. Mimi! Do something!"

Désirée grabbed the tablecloth from the next table over, intending to use it to beat out the flames, but her hand spasmed, dropping the cloth. She bent, scrabbling to pick it up, noting distantly the crackle of the flames, the rising heat in the room. The flare of the fire threw everything into sharp relief as she came up, flinging the tablecloth over the fire. She didn't see Mimi but expected help to arrive at any second. So long as the fire didn't go out too soon.

"Help! FIRE!" she screamed as she lifted the cloth to beat it again at the flames.

Only to have Mimi grab her arm. No…she grabbed her hand. The wounded one. Des went down screaming.

"Mimi, what are you doing? I need you to raise the alarm. We need help!" She gasped out the words between sobs, but Mimi wasn't listening. If anything, Mimi seemed rather…overjoyed by the whole thing.

"Let it burn!" the girl shouted, her features blurring, then coming into focus again. It was like looking through a camera when trying to adjust the lens.

Désirée fought to get free, but Mimi was stronger than she expected. "Stop. What are you doing?"

"Doing?" Mimi's face slid sideways, her mouth was an open cavern, a maw of darkness. Her eyes disappeared.

"Oh god, this isn't... FRANCOIS!" Des threw herself backwards, landing hard on her backside as a net of bright energy fell over her and Mimi, breaking whatever supernatural hold the other woman had on her.

Des came up fighting, kicking Mimi's feet out from under her, breaking a heel in the process. Des whipped off the shoe, throwing it at the monster's head, missing and nearly hitting Francois who stood half hunched over on the opposite side of the table throwing everything he had into the strands of silver and gold binding the creature between them.

The cavalry had arrived...but he didn't look so good.

Chapter 13

Désirée

T HERE WAS A BRIGHT flash of light as a second table caught. The smoke was real, becoming thicker by the minute. Did that mean it was an actual, real fire? Des didn't know. She thought there were sprinklers in the room. Why weren't they going off?

No time to worry about that now. The creature seemed chastened, but was still fighting. Francois, despite his cocky appearance, and absolute confidence, had trouble holding the net. Des had no time to worry about the sanity or safety of her actions, but threw herself on top of the girl who became Mimi again briefly before turning into Mrs. Rothschild, then any of a dozen guests, the waitstaff...she was cycling through so many forms, it's impossible to know the real one until Des clipped her upside the head hard enough to knock the girl out.

For it truly was Mimi underneath this spectral possession, but apparently, the doppelganger couldn't animate what wasn't conscious.

Which set Mrs. Rothschild screaming from the doorway, where she'd just come in with Quinn. Though it wasn't at her daughter, or even Désirée that her wrath was directed, but the man standing next to her. "NOOOO! I told you to use whatever you needed to get the jewel, but I never gave you HER!"

In the meantime, the fire was getting out of control. The baubles on the Christmas tree were exploding one after another and Désirée was too close. She put up a hand to ward off the glass shards, as she tried to figure out where Francois was. She'd lost sight of him in the smoke.

There. Fighting with his...fists?

Francois didn't seem quite as adept with his boxing as he was with magic. Des could see him dodging punches from Quinn, but was receiving more blows than he was giving out.

Francois was in no shape to fight, and she was too far away to help.

Coughing now, Des struggled through the flames, trying to get to him. She winced when something flared right next to her and gasped when she realized that they weren't touching her. None of the flames had been touching her all along.

Des lifted her left hand and looked at it, seeing the faint green line around the edges of her glove.

Green lines.

She'd read something about auras when researching Kendis's problems. Now she struggled to remember what she'd read. An aura denoted her life force.

Francois manipulated spirit energy. The lingering traces of life force still held onto by the dead.

Was one life force as good as any other?

Désirée was no longer afraid of the fire, or the flames. She only knew she would give every bit of life in her body to end this before this hotel went up, and took with it all the guests, the staff, the innocents who would suffer all for the sake of a diamond. She threw herself through the flames, hands outstretched, planting them palm down on Francois's chest. He tumbled backwards, arms coming up, wrapping her in a tight embrace as they rolled across the floor together. They came to a stop with her atop him, straddling his form, her skirt riding up to her hip though this was no time for modesty.

It was perhaps time for one indulgence, a single token of her affection in case this truly was the end.

"You know what to do with this," she said against his lips, closing the distance to give him a kiss which held back nothing. His reaction seemed automatic. Both their lips seemed intent on devouring the other, yet breathing life into each other. Her feelings were wild, scattering all over, and arousing but focused on their connection.

She then felt the flowing of energy through her body, passing through her hands into his chest, through the connection of their bodies in the kiss until he finally shoved her aside, wide-eyed and more himself than she'd seen in days.

He surged up with a wild roar, and simply...unmade everything.

The fires went out. The doppelganger ceased in its attempts to pull Mimi upright from within by flailing her limbs about despite her being unconscious.

Quinn used that moment to pick up a chair and struck down Mrs. Rothschild with it. "It was her all along!" he shouted, but no one was listening because the sprinklers suddenly went off, along with the alarms. In the noise which followed, the world descended on the ballroom while Désirée picked herself up slowly from the floor, noticing in surprised wonder that when she pressed her right palm against the floor to lever herself upright it didn't hurt. Laughing, she peeled back the wet glove and saw only the flesh of her hand. Only a knot of flesh, fresh scar tissue, marked where the injury had been to her hand. Oddly enough, it was in the shape of a star.

She looked around to tell Francois and saw he was still busy with Quinn who was trying to lose himself in the crowd surging through the door. Somehow Francois plucked him out of the pack, set him firmly into a chair. He pointed at him saying harshly, and said "Stay," the way one would a disobedient dog they'd lost patience with.

Des wondered if she was the only one to see the threads binding Quinn in place so that he couldn't have moved if he wanted to.

Francois turned then and saw her laughing there, crossing the room in long strides until he had her firmly in his arms. He ignored the way water poured down on them from the sprinklers, the gawkers, the way Mrs. Rothschild was screaming she'd been framed...none of that mattered.

Not when Francois had her face framed in his hands, staring at her so intently it was a wonder she didn't burst into flame herself.

"NEVER. DO. THAT. AGAIN!"

He was shaking. Not from weakness or pain, but from fear. It was there in his eyes, the way he was looking at her and she understood that she'd just done something incredibly dangerous.

"Deal."

Her promise was spoken as a vow, but she had her fingers crossed as she said it. She had a feeling that from now on, her life might be very different than it was before, and it was never a good idea to make promises until you knew what game you were playing.

Instead, she wrapped her arms around his neck and kissed him because he was right there, and darn it, a man shouldn't hold you like that unless he intended to follow through with the good stuff. He seemed oblivious to the way her hair rose up and coiled on its own from the water. His hands captured her face and head, holding her to him.

Which was great until the Christmas tree fell over and every candle in the place simultaneously turned off, plunging the room into darkness in the same instant Mimi woke up screaming, demanding to know what was going on.

Which made it a very good time to leave.

Maybe the ghosts were on their side after all.

Epilogue

F RANCOIS TOSSED HIS BAG in the back of the car. He turned then and headed back to the entrance and took some of the items Des was loading into hers. The weekend had been a disaster, at least from the perspective of the party. At least the police had believed their story that Mrs. Rothchild had begun the fire as a decoy to steal the diamond meant for auction so she could collect the insurance money for it. The fact that Des was now getting credit for saving the stone was going to go a long way to saving the reputation of her fledgling company. She had already been getting new inquiries for her services.

"I will be glad to be done with this place." She sighed as she set Christmas decorations and boxes of party favors in the back of her car.

"*Mais oui*," Francois echoed. "Yet, there remains the mystery of who it was that hired me." He gave her a lopsided grin and a shrug. "I had thought it might be Quinn, wishing to pull me for some reason into his voodoo experiments, but he swears it was not him. I took the assignment for cash and a note...supposedly recommended by a good friend in common, but the name I was given does not exist. I do not know who it was that wanted me here."

"Well, maybe we were supposed to meet?" Des laughed and slid the last box into her car. She stepped back to look at the plantation. It felt lonely now without guests. "I understand that the place is closing."

"*Oui.* 'For repairs following the fire.'" He quoted the official reason. "But that is fine, no one will ever believe the truth of this place or what we went through."

"But who was it that dumped you in the pond? Mrs. Rothchild?"

"*Oui.*" Francois nodded. "And the doppelganger. Considering the security footage, it could have looked like anyone, taking on their traits. In fact, I highly suspect that I threw myself in the water with the lady's help."

Des took a last look at the building. "I'm sorry that they must close, but maybe its for the best. Things need to settle down a bit here. Perhaps the ghosts need a break from all the chaos."

Francois nodded and stood close enough to her to feel her body warm against his. "I shall need to talk to a friend of mine about this place. There is too much unsettled here for me to take on. Perhaps they can calm things."

"And the bracelet?" Des asked, "What was that all about? Was that a distraction, or...or a setup?"

"It is possible that my mysterious employer and the bracelet are related. Considering my...colorful past, I may have been set up for the very theft I was hired to prevent. I wish I knew for sure."

"Maybe." Des didn't sound convinced. "I suppose it makes as much sense as any of the rest of it." She opened her car door and turned to face him. "Time to go. I need to get back to New Orleans and you...I assume you have an open road you need to find the end of somewhere."

"Nothing quite so romantic as all that. I will visit friends for the holiday. Unless you would rather...?" He reached up and touched her cheek.

"This..." Des leaned into the caress, but waved at the building behind them, "this never happened. I never met you. I cannot right now…not with my business so new. Besides, how would I ever explain how we met?"

"I do not think I am capable of such self-sabotage." He reached into his jacket. "One final decoration." He held the sprig of mistletoe over his head, and she smiled. Des attempted to snatch it from his grasp and he held it over his head, just out of her reach.

"Give it here…"

"*On se fait un bisou d'adieu*," he said, simultaneously making a request and a command. His voice deepened and his eyes smoldered as he tilted his head down towards her, and wrapped her in his opposite arm, causing midnight dreams of tangled limbs and sheets to warm her as arousal coiled within her belly. Des reached up to kiss him hard and long, giving in to the moment, as his lips met hers. He opened her mouth to receive him fully, driving more sensation than she had time to deal with to pulse through her body before she could pull away. She grabbed for the mistletoe as she retreated.

"We still never met," she teased him, the sprig in her fingers.

"Never say never, *ma chéré*."

But as she stepped back out of his embrace, she was already shaking her head. "Listen, I do have to go. I have a party I need to be at tonight, it's kind of big deal…"

"Ah, blast." Francois arched back a bit. "I nearly forgot. I too have something I need to attend. It is Jason I wish to consult about this place. I think he and his fiancé would have a better understanding of all of this if he can take the time from his election strategy."

"Jason? Election…?" Des's eyes widened. "I know very few people with that name who also know something of the supernatural. His fiancée, is her name Kendis?"

"*Oui*. You know…that is the party you are going to?" Francois began laughing. "Never say never, *mon cher*!"

Francois wrapped his arms around her and gave her a hug. "I shall see you there!"

"We never met!" Des called, but she was laughing too.

He watched her drive away knowing without needing a fortune teller or any kind of reader of tea leaves that he would be seeing her again very soon.

Despite the loss of his shirt and nearly dying more than once, he couldn't wait.

Also By

AWAKENERS SERIES

If you enjoyed *Dirty X-mas Boo* you will enjoy reading the latest book

in the series:

Dirty Glances

Join Missy's Newsletter and get the prequel to the series:

Dirty Dealings

Click the link or scan the QR Code to Get Dele's story for FREE!

Upcoming Release Book Preview

Matchmade: Detective

The cauldron boiled something intriguing under the steady guidance of the three arguing women. For family gatherings, these same women would fill multiple clawfoot tubs to the brim cleaning collards, kale, mustard, turnip, and watercress greens and then cook down the brew in the same pot until it was full. For today, however, no southern-style greens simmered in the kitchen.

The smell of herbs wafted through the old kitchen. Apart from a decade-old white refrigerator and an electric stove with three new burners, the old kitchen had seen no updates in at least five decades. The cast iron cauldron simmered on the original burner, assuming the pot needed a stove eye to heat at all. Colette wasn't sure, for she had never seen the stove eye uncovered. Cabinets painted robin's egg blue contrasted with the orange linoleum countertops. A round table welcomed guests, card games and tarot readings.

Two of the sisters were twins from Grandma Minny Bell Fury, while the other was the widowed sister-in-law of the twins' older brother John. Aunts Edie and Deedee were both practical and outspoken paternal chocolate-toned twins. In their youth Edie had been lanky and tall, while Deedee was shorter and stockier. Edie was the interpreter, hearing secrets on the wind, and Deedee was a spellcaster whose words left their mark on the world. But Aunt Emma-Lee wore glamorous glasses to set off her cat eyes and golden skin. The divinator, who glimpsed both past and future, never repeated a tale in the same manner. As a result, she sparked all the trio's arguments.

"That's not how it goes," said Aunt Deedee.

"That is the way of it."

"Tell it again." Aunt Edie requested, knowing it would rile up Deedee. She stirred the pot and winked to Colette.

"I saw a handsome gentleman in the Bayou," said Aunt Emma-Lee. Despite her glasses, she couldn't see nowadays, but she still perceived the possibilities.

"You said forest last time."

"I think I said Bayou."

"Forest," Deedee argued. "Edith, isn't that what she said?" Aunt Deedee was precise with her words, while Edie had the sharpest ears and recollection. Her ability to sequence events was second only to her ability to start an argument over anything, especially with her sisters, without ever entering the fray.

"Dierdre, that's why I asked for a retelling."

"Well, it's a Bayou now..."

The women would continue like this indefinitely. How they matched anyone was anyone's guess, let alone an impossible string of perfect matches, since the day they had worked together to help a Baton Rouge single plagued by loneliness. The Fury sisters, or the Furies as they were affectionately called, had transformed the table-talk voodoo and occult practices of previous generations into a match-making business.

"I didn't come here for all this," said Colette. "Destiny just asked me to–"

"So proud that Destiny took up the arts," said Aunt Emma-Lee. "Perhaps a few others will?"

"Yes, yes," Aunt Deedee said, "Destiny Hebert's request can wait."

This was something that all the Furies seemed to agree upon, which meant Colette would leave with her sister's ingredient list only after her aunts were done with her. Every time she got involved in one of Destiny's schemes, she ended up in a mess. The last one had caused her to walk-in on her ex copying from her term paper in college. It foreshadowed the many signs that their relationship would not endure.

The odd twist was that he had broken up with her when she switched from the lucrative surgical tracks in medical school to primary care, just before she dropped out of her residency altogether in favor of naturopathic medicine. According to him, she was not the go-getter that he thought she was. Colette had always wanted to help heal and care for people, but had never thought more of her pursuit of a medical career beyond that. That is, until she was in the middle of the lessons at the hospital, learning to transplant valves and reshape and stitch breasts on cadavers. She shivered at the thought.

Her aunts were only too happy to hear she was available. "We have a window," said Aunt Edie. "Now is a good time."

Colette could hardly track the musings of three ladies puttering around the kitchen while she sat at the table playing cards with Grandma Bell. If Grandma Bell colored the whitened mass of hair atop her head, she could have passed for as young as forty if someone failed to note the somewhat weathered skin under her keen eyes.

She was a quiet woman who reveled in any chaos her daughters created. Grandma Bell considered Emma-Lee to be a daughter, and she loved and doted on all her grandchildren. Her daughter Adelle's husband, the local matriarch octoroon's son Will Hebert, was a son-in-law. They both liked it that way, but Destiny was too young to fully understand the mutual and well-intended dynamic. Ironically, Destiny took up the battle their father did not care about and battled their father to learn the practices he would prefer she discard.

"Destiny should come round more," said Grandma Bell. "But while we have you and a window, it's best we do as we wish before giving you what Destiny wants, eh?"

They knew Colette wouldn't stick around for instructions, potions, or even a card game. Colette shook her head and supposed she could stay an hour and change. Why she thought a quick visit would be possible was beyond her at the moment.

"Don't y'all have clients who need this more than me?" Colette asked. At thirty, she knew she still had time ahead of her. Her aunts were so busy with matchmaking that they didn't need to fill time with her.

"Nonsense," said Aunt Edie. She paused, listening as if she could hear more than the raucous of shuffling feet and clattering dishes. "Yup, no time like the present in your case."

"No better advertising than our own children, nieces and nephews."

Aunt Deedee had a point, but Colette had thought matching her older sister Bernadette with the druid practicing, Gaelic-speaking Scotsman was all the advertising needed after Grandmother Hebert's proclamation to one and all that Bernie was compatible with no man alive. Not that Grandmother Hebert was exactly wrong, although the Furies and Grandma Bell enjoyed seeing Grandmother put out by the match.

Alive, the moment Grandmother spoke would certainly exclude a 14th century Highlander being spirited from Bannockburn a moment before a claymore lopped his head off, as he tells it, to the Basin Street parking garage by the Saenger Theatre, where his brother's descendant was overdosing. Colette had been as shellshocked as her sister as she witnessed the event. She had attempted to stop the convulsions before one man disappeared beneath her hands, and a roaring, naked Highlander appeared and just stopped his forearm from clothes lining her sister. She would have reduced the whole thing to Bernie confusing urban fantasy romance with real-life had she not been there. Colette still questioned her understanding of Bernie's romance.

"Nothing so outlandish for you, young lady," said Aunt Edie.

"Those were desperate times." Aunt Deedee moved back and forth faster than a woman her size should, gathering snack bags into a sack.

"Put down the jack." Emma-Lee had a penchant for helping others with cards. Colette couldn't deny it when the Furies once again revealed their second sight. Sure enough, her hand held a Jack and putting it down would bring her to twenty-one.

"Dammit, Emma-Lee, let the girl play me by herself."

"Yes, Mamma Bell." Then Aunt Emma-Lee turned to Colette. "You do like someone rugged, don't you?"

"You said clean cut!"

"Deedee, I said, clean-up. I see him cleaned-up. Rather nice, actually."

"Edith?"

"What did you say?" Aunt Edie asked. "The wind distracted me."

"Those gusts again. Omens?"

"We'll have to send her to Destiny."

Aunt Deedee rolled her eyes and dropped a vial, a note, and a bag of herbs in Colette's lap with a sigh. "She better follow directions this time."

"What happened last time?" Colette asked. The Furies and Grandma Bell each lost color.

Aunt Emma-Lee was the first to recover. She picked up Colette's caramel-toned hand and patted it. "All's well. He likes curves."

About the Author

Missy Terrell lives with a fluffy rescue cat in a duplex, and has dreamed of bringing stories to life. She writes romantic suspense of any variety because she loves staying on point as much as she loves keeping people on their toes. If you enjoyed this and want to know about future stories, please leave a review. You can also reach out to Missy at author@missyterrellfiction.com.

You can follow Missy on:

Amazon

amazon.com/author/missyterrell

Bookbub

https://www.bookbub.com/authors/missy-terrell

Goodreads

https://www.goodreads.com/author/show/43715563.Missy_Terrell

Facebook

https://www.facebook.com/missyterrellfiction/

Instagram:

https://instagram.com/missy_terrell_fiction

Tiktok

https://www.tiktok.com/@missyterrell4

CraveBooks

https://cravebooks.com/author/missy-terrell